HAPPY FRIENDS

Diversity Stories

Large Print Edition

Patricia C Furstenberg

This book was written using the English UK spelling

Print Edition ISBN 9781549797255
Version: 2017-09-20
First print edition 2017
Cover Design: Marcus & Patricia Furstenberg
Independently Published

Other books by Patricia Furstenberg
Joyful Trouble
Puppy, 12 Months of Rhymes and Smiles

Connect with the author on Twitter: @PatFurstenberg
Author's website: www.alluringcreations.co.za/wp

Dedication

To my beloved husband, my
rock, and to my two wonderful
children.

CONTENTS

1 How Pete met Lizard   1

2 Little Tail and the Snow   Pg 27

3 Little Tail meets Blue   Pg 58

4 The Summer Wind and Lizard   Pg 82

5 Three friends   Pg94

6 The Blue Forest   Pg 118

7 Hide-and-Seek   Pg 136

8 The Secret of the old, bendy tree   Pg 167

9 Little Tail and Dragonfly   Pg 196

10 Something extraordinary happens   Pg 226

11 Something's cooking   Pg 251

12 Little Tail comes back   Pg 289

Joyful Trouble, sneak   Pg 333
peek

Puppy, sneak peek   Pg 339

Acknowledgements and   Pg 347
Author's Note

About the Author   Pg 348

CHAPTER 1

How Pete Met Lizard

Each summer, as soon as the rainy season begins and the air fills with moisture, strange, unusual clouds appear in the sky.

Children and dreamers alike look towards them with excitement and wonder, challenging one another to find familiar shapes between the mists rolling above.

But they are not the only ones gazing at the sky, for in an acorn forest not too far away someone else enjoys watching the clouds go by.

And this particular morning made no

exception. Someone was, again, stomping through the forest. Which forest?

The one where the mighty oaks often make it rain with acorns. This peaceful Woodland, which can be found closer than you could imagine...

Branches pushed and snapped. Pulled by their stalks through the force of the passing-by shape, acorns poured to the ground only to crackle and pop, squashed by the moving mass.

An undefined figure made its way towards the clearing as it did every morning since the beginning of summer. Closer and closer it got, faster and faster it stomped until, without any fear of danger, out it burst into the open space.

All yellow; like a ginormous daffodil that suddenly popped up into the meadow.

"Zduf!" And the earth shook as the giant let himself fall onto the mossy ground. Or so it felt to the nearby ants.

Pete the elephant had always known he'd been blessed with an exceptional gift. The sort of gift that will never cease. The sort of gift which nobody could take away. An ability, a talent.

For Pete enjoyed watching the clouds go by and finding familiar shapes between the mists rolling above. He would lie on his back, because yellow elephants do lie on their backs when nobody is watching, he would rest his head on a tuft of grass and cross his hind legs.

"There..." he sighed in relief stretching his sturdy body, enjoying the velvety grass brushing his skin. And his gaze swept over the tall, endless sky.

"Hmmm, I love watching the clouds go by. Especially the morning ones! They are so thin and long and always follow each other just like us, elephants, do."

For a brief moment the sparkle in his eyes was gone and his eyelashes closed temporarily as he exhaled, his sigh carrying a deep trunk echo, causing the nearby grass blades to shiver. A ladybug held on tight, for dear life. A few ants, less fortunate, slid to the ground. For this was the effect of an elephantine sigh!

Do you now wonder what it would sound like for real? Have you ever tried blowing through a trumpet or perhaps through a tube?

Then you've heard it! The profound, echoing noise made by the trunk of such an animal.

For Pete was an elephant, but a lonely elephant in this Woodland where he suddenly found himself, one rainy afternoon.

A while ago, he couldn't remember exactly how long, a little boy forgot him and left him there.

Because, you see, Pete is a yellow, toy elephant who likes to watch the clouds go by.

"Look at that one", whispered Pete and the sound of his own voice soothed him.

Pete often chatted to himself, he felt less lonely by doing so.

"With its long, blue tail it looks just like an ice-lolly... a bubble gum ice-lolly", he concluded, licking his mouth.

Believe it or not once he really did taste ice-cream, entirely by accident. How he enjoyed it! Pete beamed at the tasty memory.

Thinking of ice-cream always made him smile.

Of course, it didn't compare to running through tall grasses pretending to swim! Now, that usually set him off laughing. How the grass tickled his trunk! Or... or to blowing over dandelion flowers and watching their little umbrellas float away. How they filled his heart with joy! And with a feeling of belonging too. For if the tiny seeds with their delicate umbrellas could grow and thrive no matter where they landed, then so could he!

"Fly away, little fellows. Safe journey!" he would call after them, waving good-bye.

Pete gave a contented nod just as another thought sprang into his mind. "What about me! You can't forget me!" the long neglected memory seemed to be calling.

Of course, the warm autumn afternoons, one mustn't forget those joyful moments!

Stepping on dry leaves, oh, how they tickled his feet! And how his loud bursts of laughter would send them spinning around!

Yes, there were so many smiles and giggles to choose from in a day!

And now, these ice-cream clouds...

Pete fanned himself with his ears while following the outline of one cloud with the tip of his trunk, shaped just like an ice-cream.

"It looks to me more like a rainbow ice-cream", a little voice buzzed out of the blue.

Pete's ears dropped to the ground and his trunk, from the highs of the sky, plummeted onto his chest, trumpeting a nasal "ouch!" Faster than you would imagine for someone his size, Pete was on his feet.

"Thump!" made his sturdy body.

His eyes were large in wonder, taking in as much of his surroundings as he possibly could, the elephant turned around and around, searching for the owner of the strange, high pitched voice. And just as his eyes seemed to have grown in size, his heart had sunk into his chest.

Pete was sure that any minute now, any minute, it will simply jump out and run away!

Because... who spoke?

No-one else was around!

At least nobody a creature as big as Pete could spot in a first glance...

"Who's there?!" asked he, his voice shaking, his long eyelashes fluttering fast, his heart pounding in his chest and Pete, Pete felt glad it was hidden deep inside where nobody could see how fast it jumped.

"Boom-chicky-bum-chicky-bum-chicky-bum-bum-bum!" it drummed.

Up and down and left and right turned his eyes.

Because Pete, although an elephant, was a baby elephant and strange noises scared him.

Clearing his throat, trying to shake any tremor away, he questioned in his bravest voice.

"Who... who are you... and how... how do you know what clouds taste like?"

It was hard for Pete to imagine that someone else could also taste the clouds!

"I thought clouds were my specialty", he murmured to himself, lowering his head. And his shoulders dropped, the tip of his trunk resting on the ground.

The strange voice, sounding less frightening and rather teeny-weenie the second time around, explained itself.

"It is I, Murphy the Lizard. I'm warming up in the sun on this small rock. Will you look down at your toes, please?"

So Pete looked down but he couldn't see his toes although he knew exactly where they were. Taking a deep breath he pulled in his elephantine tummy then peeped down once more.

At a quick glance it looked like the rock was cracked right across.

But no! There laid THE smallest creature Pete ever saw in his life! It was only now that he saw the lizard, a creature smaller than his foot, basking in the sun on a round, smooth rock.

"Hmm, maybe not as small as an ant..." he whispered thoughtfully, because he had seen ants before. Who hasn't?!

"Yes, that one's a rainbow ice-cream all right", the high-pitched lizard went on.

"Its best part has to be the top pink layer. Of course, the pink layer of a rainbow ice-cream tastes different than the pink flavour of early morning clouds. You know, those thin, long wisps which follow each other at daybreak?"

"When the sun has just woken up," the lizard went on, "and is lazily stretching its rays... At that precise moment the clouds are pink and they taste... hmm hmm..."

And to prove his point the lizard poked his sleek tongue and wiped his mouth in a super-fast motion. Then, without a moment's break, the tiny creature went on and on about clouds, ice-creams of so many different flavors that Pete, still surprised, could hardly follow.

The elephant couldn't take his eyes off the minute body which was bursting with so much excitement.

In return, the lizard's eyes were sparkling with joy, his tiny cheeks rosy with delight.

At last he could pour out his overflowing heart and share his passion for flavoured ideas with someone else! And not with a mere anybody, but with somebody just as fascinated by the tasty clouds as he was!

"And I do know what clouds taste like because I often climb to the top of the tallest tree and taste them. Like this!"

And to demonstrate his special skill the lizard poked his tongue, caught an ant and swallowed it before Pete could even blink.

Pete's eyes grew even larger, his eyebrows arching up, towards the tuft of hair growing on the very top of his head, so amazed was he by this skilful demonstration.

And a little bit frightened too, for the lizard's tongue was long and... blue!

The reptile looked up towards Pete and smiled.

The elephant looked down towards Lizard... and chose the biggest rock around. He had to make use of all his graciousness not to tumble over and squash the tiny animal as he sat. Because even though he was a yellow, toy elephant, he was still an elephant. Then, trying to make himself as small as he could manage, he began to study the interesting creature.

All in all it had four legs... like himself! And quite a long tail. Well, Pete had a tail too, not that he could always see it, except for when he drank from a water puddle. His tail was quite short, you see. But he could feel it all right, whenever he swished it from left to right or from right to left.

Pete examined the lizard further.

Imagine, both of them were built from the same body parts: a head, a tummy, a tail and four legs. Just that one was so tiny, the other one SO big. Of course, Pete had his long, powerful trunk, but the lizard had that fast, sleek tongue which seemed to be just as useful.

"Hello Murphy, it's sure nice to meet you", said Pete remembering his manners.

"My name is Pete and I am a yellow, elephant."

"Hello Pete, I am happy to finally meet you too", the lizard replied joyfully while beaming his widest smile. The corners of his mouth pulled back so much it looked to Pete that Lizard expanded his smile all around his head.

"Like a crown!" he thought. "This must be the happiest creature in the world, King Happiness!".

"Pete, you sure love talking..." Murphy continued. "I've been listening to your monologues about clouds for days on end."

At this, Pete's ears flopped covering his cheeks and his trunk, which was discreetly sniffing the lizard, dropped to the ground and just laid there. With his head low, the elephant sighed deeply.

"You know..." he begun, his voice so soft that Lizard had to draw nearer to hear him. "It's not nice to listen to what other people think. Those are private thoughts."

"Oh, please excuse me", the friendly

little creature placed a concerned paw on Pete's trunk. "It was quite hard not to, since you were thinking so loud, Pete."

"I always think like that", said the elephant in his deep, warm voice. "It makes me feel like I have company. I get lonely being on my own all the time..."

And he sighed again and the grass blades quivered a little. But nobody slid off them this time.

Murphy's paw tightened on the elephant's trunk.

Pete turned his long face towards him and the lizard smiled back his friendliest smile.

Only the concerned look in his eyes was telling the elephant that he did care.

The two of them sat quiet for a while. The lizard, with his paw resting on the elephant's trunk, the elephant looking into the reptile's eyes.

How long since he had last gazed into another being's eyes? How long since he had last heard another voice?

Too long for such a small elephant to

remember.

The elephant and the lizard sat in silence. With just the clouds, floating above, continuing to change their shapes.

The grass blades didn't shiver.

After a while, Pete concluded on a more cheerful tone.

"But I love watching the clouds go by and talking about them. Imagining how they might taste or where they might be going. Where they came from, over which exciting places they've surely floated. Just imagine!"

The elephant and the lizard sat in silence. With just the clouds, floating above, continuing to change their shapes.

The grass blades didn't shiver.

After a while, Pete concluded on a

more cheerful tone.

"But I love watching the clouds go by and talking about them. Imagining how they might taste or where they might be going. Where they came from, over which exciting places they've surely floated. Just imagine!"

And with a dreamy look over his face he glanced up, towards the sky and smiled.

In turn, Lizard glanced towards the clouds and smiled as well. Broader than Pete, for he had a wider mouth.

The two creatures contemplated the sky together and if someone would have given their silence a colour it would had been a happy one, no doubt about that.

"Murphy, look at that cloud, that one over there!" exclaimed Pete in an animated voice.

"It looks just like you! So tiny, but with a long tail behind", and the elephant quickly thrust his trunk towards a cloud floating on their left.

"And look at the other one, flying right beside it", answered Lizard.

"It looks just like you, Pete! It's even got a long nose, just like yours!"

They both burst into laughter. A high-pitched one and a deep one.

"This is a trunk!" exclaimed Pete, slowly waving his trunk from left to right, bending it and stretching it to prove its usefulness.

"It's sort of a nose-hand-straw", he described it further. "And one of the most useful parts of my body", he concluded, content with himself.

"Trunk", repeated the lizard for better remembering. He beamed at Pete.

"You know, I too love to watch the clouds go by. From now on, let's watch them together!" said lizard.

"Oh, let's!" exclaimed the elephant and his cheeks turned rosy with joy, the spark back in his eyes. "And every now and then you could climb to the top of the tallest tree and taste them. I'll tell you from down here how I imagine them to taste and you", his trunk pointed towards Murphy, "from the top most branch of the highest tree, YOU could taste them for real!"

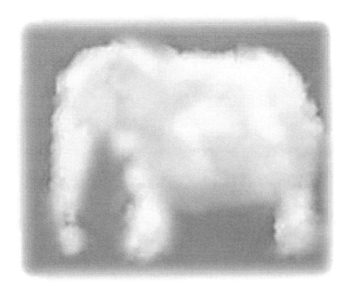

And Pete swiped his trunk in an arched movement, his eyes rolling along.

Murphy cheered stomping his feet in approval.

"Yes! And when my tummy gets too full with those delicious clouds and I won't be able to climb down anymore, you could let me slide down on your long trunk and lay me back onto my rock to have my siesta in the sun!"

Right at that moment two clouds, shaped like two smiles, floated above their heads across a sky painted in shades of ice-cream.

And it is said that from that day on, the two new friends, Pete the yellow toy elephant and Murphy the tiny, friendly lizard shared many tasty moments seated next to each other on their Rock.

Watching the clouds go by and chatting.

All day long.

Together.

CHAPTER 2

Little Tail and the Snow

"Mighty oaks from little acorns grow." Or so says the old proverb.

Not many know, but as early as the second week in autumn there is always an acorn seed brave enough to let go of the branch on which it sprang during spring and had grown throughout summer.

Taking nothing with itself but its green jacket and scaly hat, it falls.

Down and down it goes.

Its green jacket and scaly hat are

more than enough to protect the stout body until it will find a place just right for the mighty acorn tree found within its heart to finally spring and grow.

The morning was a warm one and the acorns have been daring each other long enough. It was time for the first one, the bravest one, to let go.

Mind you, the bravest doesn't have

to be the biggest one.

There is a sudden rustle through the branches and, yes, down, down the acorn falls, right onto a pile of soft leaves.

Its adventure has only just begun.

In the very same Woodland, only a few trees away from the falling acorn and not too far from the Rock on which Pete the elephant and Murphy the lizard enjoy sitting and watching the clouds go by, there lives a reddish-furred dog known by the name of Little Tail.

His cosy home, nestled inside the hollow of an old, friendly oak is simply furnished.

He has a bed laid with dried leaves for warmth, a table by the window and a few shelves which are always stuffed with provisions.

Of course, he also has a cooking pot, two tea cups which double up as soup bowls and two plates craftily carved out of nutshells.

And he has one leafy book titled The Book of Life.

Little Tail's best-est best friend is the Summer Wind and their favourite past-time must be watching the sunset together.

That's because sunset time is the Wind's longest break from his daily job of blowing up and down the Woodland's paths. And it is during this particular time of the day that the two friends enjoy each other's company the most. So much so that they can do nothing at all but sit together, silently watching how the sunset paints the sky.

Recently though, Little Tail had been visibly absorbed by his own thoughts. He would still sit next to his friend, like always, but his head would be tilted thoughtfully and, every now and then, he would nod without apparent reason. And then he would sigh.

Not deep and nasal like Pete's.

Little Tail's sighs were guttural, coming from the back of his throat and they made his whiskers tremble and the fur in the front of his neck shiver in small waves.

"Today's sunset is not like yesterday's one", the Wind would whisper.

"U-hm", would murmur Little Tail, his gaze cast far away.

"The sunset is more orange today, while yesterday's one was bright pink", the Summer Wind would go on.

"U-hm", Little Tail would mutter once again.

"Oh dear, now the sunset's green! I think the Sun's sick..." the Wind would test the waters one last time.

"U-hm", was all that Little Tail would answer, completely lost in thoughts.

"Well then, good morning Little Tail, I hope you had a nice breakfast for a sleep", the Summer Wind would try one last time to break through his friend's day dreaming.

Or is it sunset dreaming?

Usually right about now Little Tail would realize he's been drifting off again and, in a sorrowful voice, he would apologise to his friend for not paying attention to their conversation. The small dog knew too well the Wind's kind heart and could feel, rather than see, that his blustery friend was concerned for him.

But what could Little Tail do? He couldn't shake it off, like one would do with water.

For sadness wasn't something he could touch. And he wasn't really sad, was he? More of a nag in his chest, a longing feeling.

Casting his look far over the hills Little Tail would sigh his deepest sigh.

"I'm sorry, Wind. I just can't find my peace anymore", he finally explained himself one evening. "I feel like something's missing, right here", and he touched his chest with his paw right where his heart was.

Then he gazed far away and his snout quivered. Maybe because of a scent he might have caught; maybe in anticipation.

"I want to see the Snow..."

The Summer Wind had never, ever seen Snow. He had never even met someone who had actually seen Snow. Honestly, he was getting the chills just thinking about it, **SNOW**!

That's why Summer Wind couldn't even begin to imagine what Little Tail talked about; nor what he longed for...

But Little Tail was his best friend – or what else would you call someone you share each evening with, sitting and watching the sunset without the need to exchange a word and still having the best of time? And Summer Wind, more than anything else, did not want to see his friend sad. But he didn't want to see his friend go away either, especially in search of something that might not even exist!

So during the past few days, through his good heart and happy nature, every time Little Tail was sad and thoughtful the Wind, taking a deep breath, would blow over the blossom trees.

In an instant, white and pink petals would flow in gentle swirls around the dog's home.

The Wind, blowing once more, would scatter the swirls of softness all over, making them spin and spin. And right about now, with a loud and cheerful bark Little Tail, leaving his place on the porch, would madly run around his home, his tail wagging happily, "swish – swish, swish – swish", his ears bobbing.

Joining in with the gentle swirls the dog would chase them, bark at them, smell them, sneeze because of them, try to lick them and even taste them...

But eventually he would stop as if remembering something, lost in thought again, everything around forgotten.

And he would sit in the middle of the grass, partially covered by the scented layer of petals and stare over the fields and over the hills, far away, his snout quivering. And the fur in the front of his neck would shiver.

"Please don't be sad, Little Tail", the Summer Wind always pleaded with as soft a breeze as he could manage to whisper. "Look around you, there is as much snow as you could possibly wish for. See how tall and green the trees are and how blue the sky is, peeking through their branches? Can you feel the sunset slowly warming up your fur? Listen to our Woodland getting ready for the night... These are all familiar sounds and places and I am here too. Why would you want to go away, in search of something that might not even exist?"

Little Tail would just exhale, lost into the sunset. And his own thoughts.

The Wind would then softly blow one last time, in a gentle embrace.

"Oh", Little Tail would sigh again and his voice would be as soft as a secret he wished to keep to himself. "You are right, Wind."

His head suddenly lowered, his snout close to the ground, his floppy ears dangling on each side of his head, causing the fur to fold in layers over his forehead, Little Tail was the picture of concentration. His tiny paw scraping through the petals covering the ground.

Then his head would suddenly bob up, his ears dangling backwards, pulling the extra layers of skin away from his forehead.

The Wind would now see the twinkle in his friend's eyes and he would hear the sudden excitement in his friend's voice as everything would come out in one breath.

"But I HAVE to see the Snow... I

shall not be long. I'll come back... as soon as I've caught a glimpse of her! I just HAVE to see what Snow looks like. Is she really as white and as bright as they say? Is she really that cold? What does she feel like? What if she, too, is alone, waiting for a friend? You see, I just have to find out! I HAVE to!"

Until... early one morning when the leaves were still sleeping in the trees and the morning birds were only stirring up a little, almost getting ready to wake up but not quite, everything else still peaceful and quiet.

With a shiver of anticipation Little Tail set off on his adventure to find Snow.

His parcel well stuffed with food and his warmest scarf around his neck, the red furred dog shut the door with a swipe of his tail and... off he went!

He walked and walked over fields and over hills, walked while there was daylight and rested at night, walked towards the place where he knew he would find Snow: up North.

And for quite a bit of his journey, whenever he felt just a little bit lonely a warm breeze made its way around him.

It was the Summer Wind letting his friend know he is not completely alone in his adventure.

Thus until one morning when, just as Little Tail jumped out of his night shelter of leaves and twigs...

"Ha-chu!" his tiny snout itched and twitched.

How thin the morning air was! How clean it felt! As if someone had washed it during the night and put it out to dry and now, now it was bright and fresh, brand new! Squeaky clean!

Little Tail twitched his nose again and gave a little shiver.

It felt exceptionally cold that morning, nippy. The small dog could almost feel the air's sharp teeth pecking at the tip of his nose and along the edges of his ears.

"Brrr", he shivered as he took a deep breath.

The air's iciness went right through his lungs. Now he felt cold on the outside AND on the inside!

But the sky was clear and blue without a single cloud on the horizon and, as if by magic, as if somebody had just turned on an invisible switch that morning, it smelled of Snow!

It smelled of clean, fresh air, of exciting, white places and of icy hopes.

Even though Little Tail had never smelled Snow before in his life he just knew this HAD to be it!

Pointing his snout towards the sky he took a deep breath, filled his mouth with air while puffing out his cheeks, holding his breath.

A mouthful of snowy aroma! His eyelashes fluttered while tears formed in the corners of his eyes as the muscles of his cheeks started to protest against the never-ending effort. But he closed his eyes, holding in the gulp of snowy air until... he finally swallowed it.

He smiled, licking his mouth.

It kind of tasted like Snow, he thought and he quickly agreed with himself. Because it tasted like nothing he'd munched on before!

His cheeks turned red and the tip of

his nose, the part that reached the furthest away from his head, turned red too.

"Hello, Snow!" he shouted at the top of his voice as he opened his eyes. "Hellooo!" joined in his body with a sudden jump.

All was quiet. Not one voice

answered back. Not a bird stirred in the trees, nor a branch twitched.

"Hello, Snow!" called Little Tail again, louder. "Hellooo!" called his body again with another bounce.

The silence around him felt so thick that the small dog was sure he would be able to touch it. It seemed to be never-ending and un-breakable.

Still, Little Tail didn't give up. He had finally found the place he'd been looking for, now he just had to be patient and wait for Snow to show herself.

Giving a small shiver Little Tail picked up his parcel and observed his surroundings with a knowing eye.

If he was going to spend some time here, in the Snow's company, he had better find himself a proper shelter!

It didn't take him more than three

blinks to find exactly what he was looking for.

"Last night I probably fell asleep right on the doorstep of my new home", he laughed at himself noticing the round entrance of what looked like a tree hollow.

He studied the opening, his whiskers quivering in anticipation. A bit rough around the edges, but that was a good sign it wasn't used. Still, just to be on the safe side Little Tail knocked gently while his own heart throbbed a little faster. Waiting three blinks he knocked again, this time in the rhythm of his own heartbeat.

"Nobody!"

With the thumping of his own heart still echoing in his ears the dog took a first step inside his new home, sniffing cautiously.

"Dry and clean, every home-owner's dream!"

Little Tail spent most of the morning cleaning and furnishing his new shelter.

First he found a piece of bark wide enough to use as a door. Then, holding a few twigs in his mouth, he swiped the floor clean and built himself a proper bed with sticks and lots of dry leaves for both softness and warmth.

Out of a squashed acorn covered with a smaller piece of tree bark he improvised a table and, while dusting off the walls, he discovered that he even had a small window, for some extra light! Of course, he will have to make himself a curtain or it will never do!

To finish off his furnishings he placed three small rocks together as a stove and gathered three acorn shells to use as food containers. For one must never forget the food supplies when one is, indefinitely, waiting for Snow!

And when evening came Little Tail, giving out a sigh of relief, looked around, grateful for his cosy burrow.

He had spent the morning fixing up his shelter and the afternoon calling out for Snow while waiting for an answer and now he was tired, very tired. His paws ached and his back felt tender too and there was a little tickle in his throat every time he swallowed. But he had a warm shelter for himself and a cosy bed in which to curl up and snore until the morning... or until Snow showed up.

And that night, during his deep sleep, he called for Snow again.

"Hello!" he would say.

"Hello, hello!" Snow would answer.

And in his dream they would call and

cheer each other for they'd finally met. And they would happily run together through the icy air, chasing one another all around his new burrow.

"Good morning, Little Tail", a gentle, mysterious voice woke him up.

Little Tail will always remember that special morning.

As soon as he opened his eyes and looked outside the window, to his astonishment, he discovered that, throughout the night, a fine and delicate coating had been cast over the entire landscape!

"Oooh", he gasped and within a heartbeat he was at the door, pulling it open, his heart pounding, his body frozen in surprise.

A perfectly white carpet had been laid in front of his home too, stretching as far as his eyes could see.

The shrubs were wearing round, white hats, the fields were covered with white, fluffy mantles and just about everything else looked like it came out of a sweets factory!

"A very cold sweets factory!"

Closing his front door Little Tail turned towards the window, cautiously sniffing at the white fluff layered over his window sill.

"Ha-chu!" he sneezed. "That was cold! Wet too! And it tickled!"

The dog's eyes were wide open, filled with curiosity, his whiskers twitched. With the cold or of excitement? Probably both.

Little Tail's eyes darted between each and every shrub he could spot and even craned his neck to look up, towards the heights of the tallest trees.

Was everything covered in white?

"Everything!"

A feeling of wonder took over his heart.

"Could this be it? Could this be Snow?" the dog asked himself as quietly as possible, not daring to intrude upon the forest's silence.

He did not dare blink either, he did not dare move. Then he remembered his dream. What if this, too, will prove to be just a fantasy?

His heart thumped inside his chest and he quickly covered it with his paw, afraid the noise would disturb the silvery silence.

What if he's still dreaming?

How could he tell if he's still awake?

How...

"Good morning, Little Tail!" the mysterious voice spoke again and this time her whispers seemed to be coming from high above, together with lots and lots of delicate, white flakes falling straight from the sky!

Fluffy and sparkly, just like the ones on his window sill. Little Tail remembered how they tickled his nose. Will they tickle his feet if he stepped on them?

The tip of his tail swished a little.

His whiskers trembled, this time in excitement.

He had to find out!

Running to the door he opened it and, cautiously, put one foot forward, barely touching the white carpet, waiting.

Will it tickle?

He shut his eyes tight in anticipation, for he was a very ticklish dog. But it did not tickle. It felt... soft and, upon opening his eyes again he saw, in amazement, how his foot had sunk in a little, right through the white carpet. And it now rested onto the solid ground underneath.

Glad for the solid ground, his heart thumped.

Feeling braver, Little Tail took another step, then another. Slowly, he tiptoed cautiously, stepping further and further, taking in the white, icy surroundings, enjoying this new found softness, different from everything he'd ever touched before.

And there was more, more of it falling from the sky!

IT WAS Snow!

Little Tail was lost in admiration, head tilted backwards, mouth wide open, so that everything he would see or feel would be Snow, Snow, Snow and more Snow!

"So you came", whispered Snow while throwing an entire bucket of snowflakes over Little Tail.

"Here I am", uttered Little Tail shyly, sniffing around. He tried his best to taste the snowflakes but it proved to be a tricky task, at least for such an inexperienced dog, for the snowflakes kept on landing onto his nose!

He sneezed and fell on his bottom. Luckily the soft, white blanket covering the ground cushioned his landing.

"Bless you!" the Wintry Lady whispered softly.

"Thank you!" Little Tail replied in a small voice.

"It took you quite a while", she went on, pouring more flakes over the excited dog.

"But I am here now", he answered a little louder, now happily running all over the place, burying his snout into fresh piles of snow then sneezing, again and again.

He shook the icy fluff off his snout.

"I was waiting for you", added the White Lady and more snowflakes fell over Little Tail.

"Here I am", the dog whispered again, enjoying each and every flake.

"Where have you been?" Snow asked while placing a snowflake right on top of Little Tail's nose.

"Been looking for you", answered

Little Tail with a giggle, trying to lick the snowflake off his snout.

And so, Little Tail and Snow enjoyed their first day together as well as the following ones, blowing snowflakes at each other, playing chase or just following in each other's tracks. But most of all they enjoyed each other's company.

Looking more and more like a giant snowflake himself and not minding it one bit, Little Tail felt, day after day, more and more a part of the thick, white heaven that was, unhurriedly, taking over the entire place.

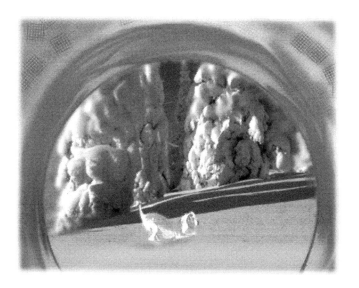

Up North.

CHAPTER 3

Little Tail Meets Blue

Friends are treasures sent to us from the heavens. The offer of friendship is a gift to be cherished and never taken for granted.

One must always remember that friends can be found in the oddest of places. One must just have faith.

Have faith in the magic of friendship and its magic will always reach you. No matter where you are or how lonely you feel.

Or so says The Book of Life.

The Snow would always start to fall early in the morning.

This is why each and every sunrise was sure to find Little Tail sitting upon an old, knobbly log, waiting for the beginning of the white flurry.

With his tail tucked underneath to keep warm and with his ears flung over his shoulders like a cape, only the dog's snout was pointing upwards, in anticipation, his eyes tightly closed.

He was sniffing at the air, listening with all his might.

"The best part of every snow fall is sure to be its starting point!" he said out loud, nodding.

Chatting like this pleased Little Tail for he almost always agreed with himself. And when he didn't, he usually ended the disagreement with a peace treaty sealed with a bite to eat. Yes, a truce, because his thinking-self, his talking-self and his listening-self preferred to get along with one another.

Smiling knowingly the dog went on, his front paws held together, his head nodding along while he explained his theory to his only audience, himself.

"The Beginning is the moment when The Very First Snowflake falls from the sky", he sighed, most sympathetically.

"Poor, Very First Snowflake, he always looks a little bit lost down here, away from his snowy friends... But then, suddenly, **THERE**!" he poked the air to his right, "and **THERE**!" he poked the air to his left, "I see another snowflake and another one and so I ask myself: wait a minute, what if this other one was The Very First Snowflake to have fallen from the sky today?"

Little Tail shook his head.

"It's not an easy business knowing exactly which one really IS The Very First!"

Then he nodded to himself, his shoulders half rising while giving a little chuckle. "It isn't an easy job!"

Eyes cast upon the sky the dog went on, his growing excitement speeding up his pace of chit-chat, the words coming out faster and faster now as the Snow fall became thicker and thicker.

"The Very First Snowflake is **EXTREMELY** important for it signifies the beginning, the very best part of the white flurry. The precise moment when the waiting in anticipation is over and it actually happens: it snows!" he recapped with a broad smile.

"Then, only then does it all start. Another silvery flake comes down and another, there and there, more and more. Oh, now it's a whole bunch of them and they are all so happy to slide down from the skies together."

"Wee!" they cheer.

"I just love the beginning of the Snow fall!" Little Tail concluded, jumping off the log.

With a content look over his face he stretched his neck, stomping his feet to warm up his short legs. Left and right, left and right bounced his paws. Left and right, left and right hopped his plump behind, his heart light and happy in his chest and, soon enough, his stout body was happily running around in zigzags.

His strong legs moved about a hundred to the dozen, his long body bouncing up and down while his long tail swished left and right, sweeping the fresh, fluffy snow.

Not long into his chase his tongue became loose, sticking out and, with his mouth half open, Little Tail seemed to be constantly smiling.

But perhaps he was. After all, the little dog had found what his heart had been longing for, and much more! Why not smile then, a whole hearted smile!

During one of these days of snowy events Little Tail began to wonder how the snowflakes actually taste!

Were they sweet like pollen?

Salty, like ants?

Or perhaps they had their own flavour, something he'd never savoured before! Something so delicious that each mouth full would be a feast in itself! And at this point Little Tail really did begin to slobber.

So early one morning the dog decided it was time he'd savour them. Not just lick and taste a few, like he'd done before. But delight himself in each and every flake landing onto his nose!

For it occurred to him that, for some mysterious reason, the snowflakes preferred, as a touchdown area, nothing better than his snout. From all the other places around!

He began by licking the very first

flake to land there. And the one right after, and the next one, without missing a single crystal landing onto his nose! For, although it wasn't a big area, maybe as large as a small cookie, it was still the main landing zone and thus it had to remain clear at all times.

The eager dog wanted to show his appreciation towards each and every snowflake skilled enough to make it onto such a small surface.

"And we have touchdown!" he could almost hear them shout.

Every now and then Little Tail would pause and look up towards the sky, admiring the flakes' unique dance before landing.

"What am I saying? Their unique trajectory before landing!" the dog corrected himself.

"They always seem to spin in light and circular leaps, like un-ending Christmas garlands hanging between sky and earth. Just look how they enjoy themselves", whispered Little Tail and he quickly agreed with himself: "yes, indeed."

All the snowflakes achieving touchdown were carefully lifted off the landing pad by the very tip of Little Tail's tongue. And, to his immense pleasure, they all proved to be pulpy and distinctly tasty.

The excited dog couldn't get enough of them!

Feet firmly tucked into the ground, head tilted backwards, his floppy ears resting over his shoulders like a cape, Little Tail would wait, greet, lick, taste and swallow. Wait, greet, lick, taste and swallow.

"Good morning", he would begin. "You are the tasty number Ten." And while saying so he would lick the tenth snowflake off his nose.

"Good morning", he would go on. "You're a tasty number Eleven, just as tasty as number Ten was, welcome!" he would greet the next snowflake making sure he spoke just as highly of each one as he had of the previous one.

Little Tail tried his best to be fair towards every single silvery flake as the last thing he wanted was an upset snowflake, especially amongst the ones piling up inside his tummy.

From one snowflake to the next one, from one chit-chat to another, joining in with the calm blizzard the evening arrived. And it found a very tired Little Tail shifting a now rounder and much stouter body onto the old log, for a well-deserved rest. He had yearned to see Snow for an extremely long time and now, when he could finally enjoy her in its entire splendour, he just couldn't get enough of it! And to top it all these friendly snowflakes had proved to be so tasty and very fluffy too.

Under the light of the new moon the dog barely looked like the Little Tail his friends back home used to know. His tummy was quite big now, growing rounder and rounder still with every fluffy, delicious snowflake he continued to swallow.

"Good evening, you're extremely delicious Mr. One Thousand Three Hundred and Eighty Seventh snowflake!" one could hear him whisper.

All the silvery flakes from high up above had already heard by now of the little dog that sits on a log, licking the snowy bits off his nose.

The news had spread that he was very polite, speaking so highly of every single one of them. So all the snowflakes now kept on looking for him and aiming for his snout to land on.

But the late descending ones, the ones falling from the sky only now, in the evening, well, these ones were in vain searching for a dog like Little Tail. Instead, all they happened upon was a funny, reddish snow figure with a huge tummy and four tiny paws, also sitting on a log while licking off each and every snowflake landing onto his elongated nose.

It was only when the snowflakes layered themselves inside his tummy, saluting one another that they began to understand: the funny-looking, snow-clothed creature was no-one else but Little Tail, the dog!

"Welcome! Welcome! How is it looking outside?" each new arrival was greeted once inside the dog's tummy.

"Still day-light?" a shy little voice wished to find out.

"Is the little dog still sitting on the log?" another one asked.

"What little dog? I only saw a strange looking snow puppet!" a late arriving flake declared.

"No no no no no! It's the same little dog, he's just been eating far too many of us!" the freshest and most up-to-date snowflake announced in a knowledgeable tone and crystal clear voice.

"Yes, three hundred and five!" a voice coming from a bottom layer confirmed.

"Five hundred and sixty-one", another one announced from close by.

"Nine hundred and seventy-seven!" a powerful one shouted.

"One thousand three hundred and eighty-nine! I am the one thousand three hundred and eighty-ninth one!" a proud voice declared.

"Two thousand!"

The ultimate number had just landed.

A frozen silence covered the entire population of snowflakes and, all of a sudden, Little Tail's spacious tummy felt quite crowded to every single snowy bit piled up inside it.

At this precise moment, while still resting on his log Little Tail, unaware of the chatting taking place inside his tummy, was admiring the snowflakes' movements in the evening light.

Their descending routes followed different pathways compared to the ones he had admired in the morning and were completely different from their afternoon glides as well.

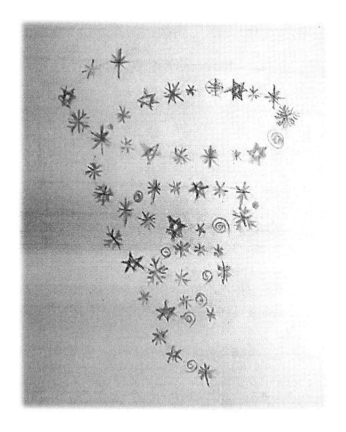

Because the evening falling snowflakes, by slowing down their free-fall, succeeded in drawing larger circles which they followed down lazily. In doing so they seemed to be saying that time had come for them all, dog and snowy flakes, to go to bed.

And suddenly in the dim, blue light of the new moon everything tasted extremely… sleepy.

"Hello?" whispered Little Tail, unsure of how to react to the stillness that seemed to have plummeted all around him.

Not one voice answered back.

"Hello in there?" he repeated softly, this time knocking onto his tummy.

Again, no answer. And in the deep, blue silence the taping on his tummy resonated loud and frosty.

It was only now that Little Tail felt the iciness compacted inside his stomach.

"Two thousand puffy, tasty snowflakes… I have eaten two thousand yummy, fluffy snowflakes…" he whispered, hardly believing it himself.

Blinking, he repeated the big number over and over again while his eyes became rounder and rounder, a big, broad smile covering his entire face.

"Wee!" running all over the place in circles, just the way the snowflakes had done all day long.

"Wee", the dog shouted again, filled with delight. "This definitely makes me a Snowdog! Hello, forest! Hello, Snow! Meet Little Tail, the Snowdog! Wee!"

But not one voice answered back. The trees were standing tall and silent, the bushes were stooping quietly and low. Not one soul seemed interested in meeting Little Tail, the Snowdog. Except for... out of nowhere, a not so little but blue character had come out to run beside Little Tail. The creature was just as tall as Little Tail but how bizarre that its shape kept changing as he hopped around.

For the excited Little Tail it didn't

matter one bit and he didn't mind either that the funny creature wasn't making a sound.

He had a play companion!

Someone to run and hop along with, someone to share his joy with. Besides, Little Tail was so excited, he felt he could chat for both of them!

And what fun they had!

Little Tail bounced and his little friend bounced too, Little Tail darted between trees and bushes, his little friend close on his heels. Little Tail ran, jumped and skied, all along the clearing, "wee!" then he rolled and "zduf!" a snow pile cushioned his landing. And his little friend did just the same, but in silence. Little Tail laughed, then laughed some more, some extra laughs being for his silent friend. The dog had a ball of a time and it surely looked like the little blue creature did too.

"I will call you Blue!" exclaimed Little Tail suddenly stopping in the middle of a loop. The blue creature nearly bumped into him, but not quite. The dog looked affectionately towards his new friend, head bent on one side, the tip of one ear touching the snow.

"Do you like this name?" he asked in

his friendliest voice, nodding his head towards his quiet companion for better communication.

His friend remained mute as usual, but was quick to nod back in agreement.

"Blue!" concluded Little Tail and then he agreed with himself. "Quite so."

And off they both went, storming into yet another round of frolicking in the snow.

Of course, not much later and the little dog was, again, dragging his short legs towards the old log. He simply had to sit and rest, yes, rest before heading for his burrow, just across the clearing.

His new friend, Blue, followed closely.

"You see", whispered the dog towards his devoted new friend, but so softly that Blue had to bend closer to hear. "Now that I've swallowed two thousand snowflakes, which of course turned me into a true Snowdog, my poor feet can't keep up with my body anymore. They tire out very quickly..." and he shook his head towards his small, round paws.

And Blue quickly shook his head too, in a most sympathetic manner.

The white forest was still and quiet around them.

The two friends were sitting on the old log, watching the evening lights being switched on one by one in the skies.

And while they were quietly resting next to each other they resembled, more and more, to creatures of the snow, one slightly red, the other one blue.

"Blue!" exclaimed Little Tail, utterly

amazed. "Just look around you, everything ELSE is blue!"

And so it was as under the dim light of the new moon the forest's shadows had just come out for their last play before bedtime.

The trees were dark blue, casting deep, mysterious shadows.

The birds huddled together, already asleep on their branches seemed painted in a similar hue.

The fresh snow covering the clearing and almost everything else Little Tail could see everywhere around him was tinted in shades of blue.

By now, the night sky had turned almost black in colour, covered in thousands of little lights and one single spotlight, the moon.

And in the middle of this fantastic setting there were two snowy creatures sitting next to each other on an old log. Two best friends moving only their heads about, looking here and there, there and here, amazed at the performance of lights and shadows that seemed to have been put on just for them.

CHAPTER 4

The Summer Wind and Lizard

You might never know the name of your neighbour down the road. But if you happen to walk the paths of the same forest with a total stranger, day in, day out, sooner or later you are bound to stumble into each other, share your likes and dislikes and, who knows, maybe even become great friends.

For friends can be made between the strangest of creatures. Just remember, you might appear to them even more alien than they look to you.

Or so says The Book of Life.

The very summer Little Tail was away searching for Snow, Summer Wind, left behind, became good friends with Lizard.

The lizard, speeding along the Woodland's corridors on the ground, had often crossed paths with Summer Wind, blustering high up throughout the trees bordering the very same pathways.

The Summer Wind, with one strong puff, would lift the most perfect leaf.

Not too young and flimsy, nor too old and wrinkled, just strong enough.

Not too long either so that its tip would just curl, slightly, when floating on the water.

And not too narrow, just wide

enough for Lizard to comfortably and safely lie upon.

Sure-footed Lizard would climb aboard this custom made boat and, like a zephyr, the Summer Wind would gently blow his breeze over the lake. And so they would drift together. Lizard on the leaf, the Summer Wind gently embracing the air around it. Tiny ripples would spread all over the lake's calm surface, all around their custom made boat, like the hems of a ball gown.

"How do you like the glide?" Wind would always want to know.

"It's most enjoyable, thank you", Lizard would answer softly, making himself one with the leaf.

The Wind would blow once again, pushing the boat further away from the shore line, the lizard slightly lifting his head. Feeling only a breeze flowing over his face he would bravely lounge forward onto the leaf.

"How do you like the glide now?" the Wind would ask again.

"It's a super glide, Wind!" a lively answer would come, the tip of the lizard's tail swishing a little, the four legged creature feeling just a bit braver on his custom made boat.

Although this was a game they enjoyed playing every time they were on the lake, on every occasion they would both pretend not to know what was next to come.

Then Wind would ask one final question.

"And how do you like the ride now, Lizard?" And with one last puff he would send the leaf riding a tiny wave far, far away, to the opposite shoreline.

"Wee!" Lizard would exclaim, his eyes shining at the bow like two signalling lights. "Wee! This is the best ride I've ever had, Wind!"

"Better than yesterday's one?" Wind would enquire further, most happily.

"Much better!" Lizard would shout back just as the green boat would reach the shore. "Much, much better, Wind! And a million thanks to you, my dear friend!"

And Lizard would laugh, his big mouth wide open, while joyfully jumping back on land. And his tail would swish madly once on solid ground, his head bobbing up and down, his long, blue tongue quickly swiping a few ants.

Then, upon exchanging friendly good-byes, they would both go their separate ways, ready to perform the rest of their individual morning routines.

It was only now, while Lizard would go in search of fresh breakfast, that Summer Wind would officially blow its "wake-up" draught throughout the Woodland.

Between us, during the mornings when the two friends swam together the Wind was running late with his daily schedule and, therefore, the entire Woodland – except Lizard – slept in.

One would think that the Sun is the one to wake up the entire natural world in the morning, isn't it?

Well, it is not so, it is the Wind. His morning zephyr blows the blankets off the sleepy animals and, by rustling the leaves in the trees, sounds the morning alarm stirring up the entire Woodland. Without his morning breeze everybody would sleep late, basking in the warmth of the early sunlight.

During lazy summer afternoons Summer Wind and Lizard enjoyed taking off together.

This time the Wind would choose a long, pointy leaf for Lizard to sit upon. Then, with a strong blow of warm air he would most carefully lift it and, together, they would soar the skies.

They would rise above the trees and the lake, above all the other earthly creatures and sometimes, in warm, quiet evenings, even above the clouds!

Lizard always liked to exclaim

"Wee!" during their take-offs, cautiously keeping his body as close as possible to the leaf. And the Summer Wind would accompany him like an echo "wee…"

Then Lizard would exclaim again, a little louder this time, most excited, "Wee, wee!" and Summer Wind, like a most trustful echo, would follow "wee… wee…"

Sometimes Lizard, feeling really brave, would even call out "Wee, wee, wee!" while ever so slightly lifting his head off the leaf. But the Summer Wind would only echo "wee… wee…"

"You know what, Wind?" said Lizard one afternoon, during their flight. "I wish we could both stay up here forever!"

"And we could navigate together over the forest and the lake and the hills and everybody looking up, towards the sky, would ask: "who are those two up there, having so much fun?" smiled the Summer Wind.

"And we would wave at them and say: wee, wee, wee, it is us, Summer Wind and Lizard!" the small reptile would complete with much excitement.

"And then, then I'd see your shadow on the ground, waving, and I'd think that it is you, Lizard, waving at me from down below", went on the Summer Wind. "And so I would wave back at you, calling your name and asking you to come up and see the world with me".

"No you wouldn't. You would know that it is just my shadow waving at you", frowned Lizard, uncertain. "For I would be sailing next to you, on this pointy leaf."

"But who would be waving at me from down below?" puzzled Wind, downhearted.

"Just my shadow", explained Lizard calmly, happy to be sailing up with the Wind.

"And where would you be then?" further asked Wind, visibly worried.

"I would be sailing up here, with you, lying on this pointy leaf", explained Lizard, trying his best to stay calm.

"And you won't be waving at me? At me, your friend?" exclaimed the Summer Wind becoming sadder with each blow.

"Yes I would! Of course I would wave at you!" exclaimed Lizard.

"Look, I am waving at you right now, see?" And Lizard, spotting his shadow on the earth below, waved frantically towards the Wind, and in doing so almost lost grip of his leaf.

The Summer Wind looked down and, spotting the lizard's shadow waving at him became very excited, an extra gush of Wind rippling through his shoulders.

"Hey, hey, hey!" he yelled, waving towards the shadow below and causing the leaf he was carrying to twist this way and that. "Hello, Lizard, my friend! What are you doing down there? Come up here and let's navigate together! Hey, hey, hey!"

CHAPTER 5

THREE FRIENDS

The time spent in company of friends will, more than once, become part of our most cherished memories, staying with us for the rest of our lives.

To laugh together, to see the twinkle of joy in a friend's eye, to comfort and take comfort in each other, to share, to sit together knowing that you thrive in each other's company, such are the joys of friendship.

Or so says The Book of Life.

In the peaceful and shady Woodland all was quiet.

Not a single leaf trembled on the branches, nor a cloud floated in the skies above.

As for the Lake, he couldn't even remember the last time his surface had been wrinkled.

The air all through, around and over the forest was so still, the entire Woodland seemed petrified. Nobody could even recall when last the Summer Wind had made his breeze felt.

Every living creature taking shelter in the Woodland was worried, wondering what happened to the Wind! Something out of the ordinary must have come over him, something terrible, to reduce him to such tranquillity.

Total stillness!

"He's missing his best friend, Little Tail", the all too knowledgeable leaves whispered to each other from the tree tops.

"Missing his friend, Little Tail", the soft grass murmured towards the rabbit burrows, which also happened to be the earth's ears.

"Missing his friend..." went the buzz throughout the forest.

"Who is Little Tail?" a freshly popped-up mushroom questioned the long eared creature bouncing about, hoppity hop, hoppity hop.

"He is the best-est best friend Summer Wind ever had", answered Busy Rabbit forced to break off his run, one back leg suspended in the air, the other one slightly touching the ground.

"And what makes him such a special friend?" the all too curious mushroom still wanted to know, causing Busy Rabbit to stop for, oh, one minute too long.

"Ah, Mushroom", sighed the rabbit and frowned, for now he had to stop from his race altogether, placing both feet firmly on the ground. "One can tell you never met Little Tail. A friend like him is like..." and the rabbit thought for another minute. "He's like the rain when there is drought. He's the shady spot you suddenly discover during a hot day's walk. He's the softest bed you crave when you are tired."

"Rain? Shade? Who's missing his bed?" asked the freshly popped-up mushroom and the rim of her large hat bounced up and down making waves of question marks.

"Haven't you paid any attention to what I've just explained?" bellowed Busy Rabbit throwing his front paws in the air in a gesture of frustration. "You're asking too many questions, Mushroom!"

And with one yank on his paw he swiftly picked the vegetable and placed it in his basket.

"And you don't even listen to the answers you receive", he concluded while hurriedly hopping on his way.

Hoppity hop, Hoppity hop.

At the same time in the Butterflies' Grassland, the true heart of this still Woodland, the Summer Wind, Pete and Lizard were having a chit-chat.

Pete and Lizard had long decided it was high time they do something to cheer up their friend, Wind. Lizard, because he was missing their flights together, their boating cruises and those special morning dreams about mysterious, faraway places. And also because, for many days now, Pete and he had long finished playing all the games they could have possibly played together!

And the summer days left ahead looked long and uneventful without the Wind's whispers and breezy jokes throughout the forest. A forest as empty as a lonely road bordered by nothing at all, not even rocks... Pete, on the other hand, because he really felt like having some more of those tasty, fluffy clouds. But without the Summer Wind's breeze no clouds were floating over the Woodland's sky. But most importantly and well above their personal reasons stood the fact that Summer Wind was their friend and they very much wanted to see him as happy and as joyful as ever. Back to his usual breezy self.

Apart from the humming made by their sporadic chat the Butterflies' Grassland was quiet, immobilized by the scorching heat, even the butterflies feeling too hot to fly about.

The three friends were the only ones sitting here, the Wind keeping his face turned away from Pete and Lizard, not wanting his friends to see how sad he really felt.

He had tried for weeks to pretend he wasn't missing Little Tail all that much but now, now, he just couldn't hide his feelings anymore. Everyone in the forest missed the friendly dog and he, he was the one missing him the most. Little Tail was his best-est best friend and that was that!

So here he was, sitting on the soft grass, embracing his windy knees with his strong, blustery arms and...

sighing

for

the

first

time

in weeks!

Profound, windy sighs.

And the forest, the forest shook with his every moan. For he was, after all, a Wind! And not before long his terrible sighs began causing havoc amongst the Woodland's animals. For nobody had ever experienced such shakiness before, such tremor.

"What is happening?"

"What's shaking the trees?"

"WHO is shaking the trees?"

"Is it a storm?"

"An earthquake?!"

"A tornado?!!"

The squirrels and the rabbits were most impacted upon for the trees' vibrations disturbed their provisions, so neatly packed into rows and rows on top of each other.

As for the beaver, he found himself

facing even more work because the tremors that took over the entire Woodland had upset the logs he'd layered, so neatly, into a dam.

"Is it a newcomer?"

"Do we have a stranger in our midst?"

"Guard our children!"

"Lock the doors!"

"Hide!"

Even Queen Bee had been disturbed in her beehive. Hundreds of bee larvae, awoken by the general tremor and commotion which took over the entire forest, were crying incessantly.

"It's just the Wind..."

"**JUST** the Wind?"

"**ONLY** the Wind?"

"**ALL** on his own?"

"Why?"

"For what reason?"

"Whatever for?"

Each and every Woodland animal, no matter how small, how deep in the ground or how high in the trees, was now deeply concerned and most impacted upon by the Summer Wind's howl-ish sighs..

So Pete the yellow elephant, with his trunk thoughtfully resting on the grass, was scratching his head trying to think of a way to bring Little Tail back. Back to their Woodland home.

Right next to him but on a rock, an ordinary rock, not the Rock, sat Lizard, also thinking, his tail swishing slowly.

"Swish... swish..."

"Since Little Tail left nobody barks my name anymore", Lizard's clear voice rose over the clearing. "Let's DO something!" he exclaimed suddenly, his tail picking up the pace.

"Swish - swish. Swish - swish."

"We've got to bring Little Tail back." Lizard was always ready for action, always on the move and his thoughts were very much like his speedy, agile body.

"There is nothing to be done", whispered the Wind and he sighed again and the entire Woodland trembled along.

Somewhere underground a voice

complained.

High up in a tree a hatchling cried.

But down below Wind still wailed on.

"Nooobody can bring Little Tail back... It's been soooo long since he left... eeeven his scent has faded awaaaay from the Woodland! Uuh, ooh!"

And the forest shook.

"Oooh! Hooow I wish I could be the ooone to go Uuup North! But I'm ooonly a Summer Wind. My strength would ooonly take me as far as the Autumn's Territories", he howled further, pointing towards his right where the Autumn's Territories were meant to be.

"Little Tail wooon't even hear my whispers from there; he's toooo far away, up North. Ooooh!" and his voice died away, overcome by sorrow.

"Wait a minute there!" exclaimed Pete, his eyes alight with excitement, his cheeks flushed.

The Summer Wind's arm froze in motion, outstretched towards his right.

The elephant gave a quick laugh.

"No, I didn't mean to play freeze, not right NO-OW. You just gave me an idea! What if we send someone? With a message! For Little Tail!" Pete's trunk poked the air, pointing towards the sky and his voice boomed with enthusiasm.

"Send somebody?" questioned the Wind not sure who that someone could be.

"Send someone!" agreed Lizard in an animated voice, putting on his broadest smile. "Of course, Pete is right!"

"But who would want to go that far North? That far away into the c-c-cold?" whispered Wind already feeling a chill going through his windy shoulders.

"Well, we'll just have to think that one through", concluded Pete and his trunk dropped, searching wishfully through the tufts of turf, as if looking for an answer. Perhaps the answer lay between the blades of grass?

A few heads quickly slid underground.

But Pete needn't search long as the quick thinking Lizard came up with an idea.

"I know who! I know who!" he shouted at the top of his lungs, his tail swishing madly behind him.

A few heads dared to peek out of their shelters.

"There IS someone who CAN travel such a distance. Someone who HAS travelled up North before and who won't get too c-c-cold up there either!" came the answer while Lizard hopped triumphantly on his short legs, doing a happy dance. He watched his friends with sparkling eyes for he now knew that their problem was solved. He felt so thrilled, he felt as tall as Pete and as light as the Wind! He smiled again and it looked like he was wearing his smile all around his head.

"King Happiness indeed", Pete thought to himself.

"Swish - swish, swish - swish", the lizard's tail quickly moved about.

Pete and Wind were too astonished for words. The witty Lizard had taken them both by surprise.

The elephant's eyelashes battered fast over his big eyes, his mouth half open, his little tongue hanging loose.

The Summer Wind's shoulders stopped their tremor and he even forgot to sigh. They were both as still as the Woodland, staring at their friend, anxiously waiting for the Grand Announcement.

Who could possibly be The One willing to deliver their message to the long departed Little Tail? Who could it be? Someone they all knew, someone who had already travelled up North before? And would agree to travel there AGAIN?

"Who?!" demanded Pete, tongue still hanging.

"Who?" the Wind's eyes questioned in silence.

"Who?" replied Lizard with a knowing smile.

The lizard's heart was bursting with happiness. He could hardly contain himself, thrilled as he was by the realization that his dear friend, Wind, would be in high spirits once again. More than anything else Lizard loved to make his friends happy. And when his friends were happy, he was happy too.

Moving his excited glare from Wind to Pete and then to Wind again, Murphy finally explained himself.

"Well, the clouds, of course!"

Pete looked up towards the clear, blue sky. "The clouds...?" he repeated, not so sure he quite understood his friend's plan.

High above their heads there wasn't a cloud to be seen. Nor had there been any during the past... well, many days, too many for a toy elephant such as himself to be able to count. But the Summer Wind, who knew his friend's mind all too well, smiled for the first time in weeks for he had understood Lizard's plan.

Jumping to his feet he took a deep breath. And while Pete was still trying to figure out how their plan would work, the Wind was already busy blowing.

Gently at first, for he was a gentle wind, then gradually stronger and stronger, especially over the lake. And, imagine this, before Pete even knew what was happening, clouds started to form across the bright blue sky! Small, almost shy ones at first, yet constantly changing, becoming greater in number and larger in size.

"There!" exclaimed the Wind content with himself and his face was happy and pleasant once again, although quite red from the effort.

And Pete smiled too for he had finally understood Lizard's plan. Lizard watched Pete with a twinkle in his eye. The yellow elephant winked back at his cloud-tasting friend and they both set to work.

Lizard, perched on the top of the tallest tree while Pete was lending an expert eye from the grass down below. Lizard shaping the clouds with his sleek and skilled tongue, while Pete was checking that all the letters were in their right places.

"LITTLE TAIL, PLEASE COME BACK HOME!"

was soon written across the sky above in cloudy letters.

Without another word Summer Wind blew one last, final blow and the message took off, swiftly soaring towards the faraway place where Little Tail found himself: Up North.

"One done", nodded the Wind approvingly. "Many more left to go." And with deep, rapid blows he set to crafting more clouds.

"More?" wondered Pete.

"More!" smiled Lizard from the top of the tallest tree.

"Much more!" agreed a happy Wind.

Now three smiling friends were sitting together in the Butterflies' Grassland, waiting excitedly.

Wind was happy, Lizard was excited while Pete was both hopeful and tired. By putting their minds together they'd come up with a fantastic solution to their problem. Even more so, they had a plan on how to bring back their long departed friend and, thus far, the plan was working! And they'd made it work together.

Watching the cloudy letters float away the Wind gently laid his blustery arms around his friends' shoulders in a warm, summer-breeze embrace.

And it is said that from that day on all the Woodland inhabitants had peaceful lives once again

CHAPTER 6

The Blue Forest

Every place has its secrets. Some will always remain hidden, while others are just waiting for the right person to unravel them. And that person might just be you. But you will only find out if you are willing to follow your dreams.

At times you might feel scared of what lays ahead, of the unknown. But so many more times you will be thrilled and the discoveries you make will enrich you in countless ways.

And, who knows, you might even

make a friend along the way.

Or so says The Book of Life.

Underneath a quilt of snow the Blue Forest was still sleeping when, like a giant snowball, morning rolled in.

"Crunch, crackle", it made as it rolled along.

"Thud!" echoed through the sleeping trees as a heap of snow fell from a branch.

All by itself?

No, something had caused it to fall, because something... or somebody had shaken the branch it was sitting on.

"Whoosh", the breeze sang as it bounced against the tree trunks.

"Whoosh... shhh... shhh."

Something... or somebody had stirred it.

"Thump!"

The furry snowman jumped off the log. He danced a little jig. He felt happy and ready to play.

With so much snow around, what else was there to do? He rolled himself into a ball and bounced about.

"Thump, thump, thump." And before he knew it a second snowman came out of the shadows and, rolled himself into a blue ball, faithfully following him around.

The first snow-ball, the fury one, went "tuff, tuff, tuff" around the trees, its excited bounces softened only by the thick layer of snow.

The second snow-ball, the blue one, followed closely.

but overlooked a sapling, lost its balance and… "thump!" the two snowballs collided with each other.

"Thump, thump, thump..." echoed the forest, bumpy echoes spreading further, bouncing off the frozen trees.

"Thump, thump, thump!"

Little Tail opened one fuzzy eye, still half asleep from his bouncy dream.

"Thumping? What a funny dream to dream. And now it's thumping at my door."

He closed the eye again. Perhaps the thump will go back into his dream, where it came from.

But the persistent knock came through again.

It was at his door, it travelled through his room, it tickled his ear.

"Thump!"

"Thump!"

"Thump!"

Little Tail yawned and stretched and, ever so slowly, rolled out of bed. Putting one small step ahead of another he headed for the window. Just a peek and he'll spot whoever was outside his door.

The light pouring through the small opening was too bright, like thousands of diamonds shining in the sun. The sleepy dog had to shade his eyes.

"What is this?!"

It was only on his second attempt

that he managed to spot it. Not the source of all the thumping, but the source of the bright light pouring in.

It was the Snow, glimmering in the sunshine!

Little Tail's eyes shone with pleasure.

"Oooh!" he exclaimed and his heart bounced with joy, his tail starting to move slowly. "It's still here! The Snow is still here!" shouted the dog jumping madly about his burrow, his long tail now wagging a hundred to the dozen.

Now his front paws touched the floor and, with his bottom in the air, his tail wiggled to the left.

Now his back paws were on the floor and, with his front paws in the air, his floppy ears swinging backwards, his tail waggled to the right.

Left, right; left, right...

"It did happen! It did happen!" he sang, feeling just as happy now as he'd been the moment it first snowed.

Wiggle, waggle...

"I did meet Snow! I did! I did! I..."

The wiggle stopped, the waggle suddenly froze as a new thought sprang into Little Tail's mind while all was quiet again in the little burrow.

Carefully, very gingerly, he felt his tummy. Then a sigh of relief was heard and the dog nodded in approval. His tummy was still nice and round!

"I did eat snowflakes!" he exclaimed. "Ooo, I did turn into a Snowdog... or was it a Snowball?" And his tongue made a quick swipe over his nose as he remembered the two thousand snowflakes he'd been licking off the night before.

Then a peculiar memory, rather bouncy and friendly, came forward.

"Blue!"

The name seemed to fill the room.

"Blue?"

The question followed, bouncing off the walls.

What happened to Blue? Had he disappeared overnight? Where to? Or maybe, maybe he's still fast asleep? Perhaps somewhere around here?

"Blue..." Little Tail whispered while his eyes searched all around the narrow burrow he now called home.

A cosy little bed... the dog shook his head.

"No, no space to hide underneath."

His eyes moved further, his eyebrows arched in question - The small stove?

"N-no, no space behind it either."

His eyes swept past his few pots and cups, his hands lifting a couple of nut shells. "Nobody!"

He even searched underneath his tiny table, but no-one was sleeping under there either.

"Thump, thump, thump."

Outside his door!

Little Tail's snout twitched.

"Who's there?" he asked in half-whisper. "Blue, is it you, my friend?"

But no-one answered. Only the door seemed to shake as the rattling sound filled the small room.

Little Tail felt the vibrations brushing over the hairs at the back of his neck, causing them to stand. He shivered, because he was a ticklish dog, of course.

Then, taking a cautious step towards the door, he waited. Will it shake again? Was somebody trying to break it down?

Summoning up all his courage he took another step forward.

"Think good thoughts and good will come to you", Little Tail remembered the old advice.

"Surely someone shy, but very persistent is outside... I better invite them in to warm up." And with a faint smile Little Tail opened his door.

Who was it, knocking on his door?

He blinked, again and again.

Standing in the doorway, the pleasant warmth of his room behind him, Little Tail felt only the wintry chill rushing in. No-one else.

Nobody was standing outside his door.

"Blue?" he called.

Silence.

Outside the air was frosty and the Snow was bright.

Inside there was only himself... and the rapid thumping of his heartbeat.

"Curious", whispered the dog and his eyebrows went up in wonder. His right front paw went up too, as if to ask a question. The hairs at the back of his neck were still standing.

Closing the door Little Tail gave a shiver and jumped into bed. He rolled himself into a ball, enjoying the soft layers of dry leaves and soon felt warm again. He shut his eyes, but his dream wouldn't come back.

Something else was on his mind.

"Blue... Where could Blue be? Could he be outside? Too shy to speak so he ran away when I opened the door? Surely if it was me there, in the freezing, winter morning, feeling too shy to speak up, I would be so happy if my friend would come out looking for me, invite me in to share a hot cup of tea and a friendly chat. I would be so happy if that happened to me."

And with a nod of agreement Little Tail jumped up, stirred the fire, put on his tiny tea pot, prepared two nutshells and, when the water was just right, crushed a few fir leaves inside for a good winter's brew. Then, with his scarf tightly wrapped around his neck, he stepped out the door, determined to find Blue.

"First things first", he laid out his plan while stomping his feet to keep warm. "I should do a quick search around my burrow."

But his plan proved easier said than done for the fresh snow covering the ground was deeper than it looked. Soon the search became a long and strenuous exercise.

The old tree was thick and its trunk

was knobbly. One couldn't keep walking right next to it, so at times Little Tail had to go out of his path, furthering away from the trunk in order to avoid a lump or a root, thus lengthening the walk.

Upon reaching his front door again the little dog paused for breath. His heart was pounding, his legs were aching.

"And not a trace of Blue..."

The sadness in his voice echoed far away through the crisp morning air.

"Blue... blue... blue..."

Little Tail listened to the sound of his voice being carried away, the only noise between the snow-cushioned trees... All was silent again.

And then, somewhere, a branch snapped.

Was it Blue or just the weight of the

Snow piled on it that caused it to break?

Little Tail waited, but nobody came through.

With a heavy sigh the dog stepped inside his burrow. He sat himself at the window, a steaming cup of tea by his side.

His heart was sad, but his mind was determined to keep watch, sure in his belief that Blue would show himself.

Sooner or later...

That entire day Little Tail sat at the window, drinking hot tea and gazing into the woods.

The steam rising from his cup warmed his cheeks and tickled his snout while the fresh aroma of fir leaves reminded him of another woodland, left far behind, a place with tall, green grass and fast streams, warm raindrops, happy splashing and dear friends, long missed, not a moment forgotten.

"I remember..." Little Tail whispered to himself, smiling.

And his entire face beamed a different smile for each and every memory from back home.

His eyebrows went up when he thought of the tall acorn trees with cool shade.

And Little Tail took another sip of tea. His cheeks quivered when he thought of Wind, blowing gently a wake-up call, each and every morning. Gentle, strong Wind.

"Here's to Wind!" he exclaimed as sipping once more.

His ears flopped and fanned as he remembered Pete, the friendly giant toy elephant, always seeing the best and seeking the best in each situation and each soul he encountered. Brave Pete.

And he sighed, then took another sip of tea for Pete's sake.

His tail swished remembering Murphy the Lizard with a long, blue tongue and a wide smile, King Happiness, as Pete used to call him. Happy Lizard.

And the last drop was drunk for Lizard.

And the last drop was drunk for Lizard.

CHAPTER 7

HIDE-AND-SEEK

Waiting is a virtue for it requires patience and determination while, at the same time, one must stay focused on the target and have faith in oneself.

Now and again it might feel like waiting is a waste of time, but one must persevere for those are the moments when your endurance is being tested and strengthened. Those are the times when a strong character is being built.

Or so says The Book of Life.

All day long Little Tail had sat by the window sipping tea, dreaming of the past and waiting for his friend, Blue.

Lost in thought, he raised the cup yet again but this time no liquid came out. Cushioned in his paws the nutshell felt warm, giving out a refreshing aroma. The dog sniffed the beloved scent, tilting the cup even more, hoping for one last drop of tea. Back went his head, up went the cup until, head completely backwards, the cup was resting with its rim flat over the dog's face. But the rear motion threw the greedy creature off balance sending paws and tail flying through the air.

Dog and nutshell fell to the floor.

"I'm all right!" Little Tail's voice rose. "Look at the bright side, I always say", he continued while picking himself up, "an empty cup means no spills".

It was only after he replaced the cup on the table that he saw it.

The shadow looming outside his window.

A growl formed in the back of his throat only to be dissolved into a gush of air that made his floppy cheeks quiver. Whiskers twitching. Little Tail was all eyes.

When did that happen?

When had the tiny silhouette crept outside his window?

How long had it been standing there for? Watching him...

Oh, but did it really matter!

The dog's mouth opened like it had a mind of its own, showing off a huge smile. His tongue rolled out in excitement. His tail, which at first had just stirred a little, was now wagging in full swing. So much so that even Little Tail's plump behind was shaking.

The dog knew the silhouette outside only too well: small, round, with four tiny paws...

"Blue!"

And the name burst out of his mouth at the same moment his front paws began waving frantically. It looked like the over-excited dog was making use of every extremity of his body to draw his friend's attention.

"What should we do first?" So many questions raced through Little Tail's mind, chasing one after the other.

"Run outside and frolic in the snow? Share a cup of tea inside? Ask Blue where had he disappeared to last night? Where had he been this entire day? A day twice as lengthy and trice as forlorn when passed without a friend. What took him so long to show himself again? Does he want to play?"

"But of course he wants to play!" exclaimed the dog, waving again.

And Blue waved in return.

Jumping and signalling Little Tail called out, "Blue, my friend, you're back, you're back!"

And outside, Blue bounced and gestured in return.

"Come in!" Little Tail beckoned his

friend.

"Come here!" gestured Blue.

"Oh!" Little Tail was beside himself with joy. "Blue does want to play! Here I come, Snow Games!"

The dog's tongue was hanging out in excitement as he rushed towards the door. Throwing only a glimpse through the window he noticed Blue, also running towards it. But half way into his run, in a rush of paws, floppy ears and wagging tail, the dog remembered his scarf, left by the window. Spinning on his heels he chased back to grab it when... he stopped dead in his tracks.

"Imagine that!"

Outside, Blue too was hurrying in the same direction, back!

Little Tail waved and Blue waved in return holding his own scarf, just as the dog held his.

The dog stared at the sight.

"Blue, wearing a scarf?! Oh, he's letting me know that I, too, should wear one! What a thoughtful friend!" And with a big grin on his face Little Tail waved his scarf, calling out, "Yes, yes, I do have it! Thank you! I'm coming out right this minute to play!" And in his eagerness he jumped in front of the window just like Blue bounced outside.

Dog and friend, they both darted towards the door.

To play with Blue again! To run and frolic in the snow with a friend, Little Tail couldn't wait for all the fun to recommence!

"Here I am, Blue!" he called as he opened the door.

In the late evening hour the light

pouring through his door drew a bright half circle onto the Snow. Having just emerged from his well-lit burrow and into the twilight the dog needed to blink for a second or two for his eyes to adjust to the dim light outside.

He only blinked once, twice ... maybe three times. Blink, blink, blink and...

TA-DA!

Finally! There was Blue! Not quite in the middle of the bright patch, rather near its edge, peeking from a shady corner. Unsure, perhaps, of the beam of light shining from a burrow on the ground and looking as bright as the moon on the sky?

Or perhaps he was just shy.

"Blue!" called Little Tail, bouncing up and down on his door step.

And the word rolled out into the dark

forest, "Blue, blue, blue…"

"I am so happy to see you, Blue!"

"Blue, blue, blue…" echoed the trees again.

Perched on his spot, Blue hopped and waved his arms at Little Tail, silently, of course. But this quiet behaviour did not bother the dog, already used to Blue's silent ways.

Without wasting another second Little Tail darted towards his friend. But as soon as the dog took his first step Blue seemed to have decided on a game of hide-and-seek. For he took a step sideways... vanishing into thin air!

"Blue?!"

"Blue, blue, blue..." echoed the night.

The dog stopped abruptly in his tracks, the sudden halt to the rapid movement nearly throwing him off balance, threatening to roll him into a pile of snow nearby. He sniffed the air.

What had just happened? Which way had Blue run?

Little Tail craned his neck, not daring to step into the shadows. He glanced left. He glanced right, throwing but a safe peek into the depths of the forest.

"Why did Blue run away?"

The trees neighbouring his burrow were standing tall and silent in the late hour.

"So many of them..." thought Little Tail, suddenly feeling small and lonely.

"Where are you, my friend?" he called out, his voice such a faint whisper that the forest didn't even carry its echo. Or were the woods feeling sorry for the lonely animal and decided to leave the echo with him, as a companion? Just this once.

Little Tail hadn't noticed all this, absorbed as he was in gathering his courage. He had to go in search of Blue!

How his heart was thumping!

Taking one deep breath the dog put one paw outside the circle of light, then another.

How his knees were shaking!

He stopped and listened.

How his heartbeat echoed into his ears!

His eyes were watchful, his ears perched, waiting for a noise, a tiny crack of a twig or the odd snap of a branch to indicate his friend's whereabouts. Perhaps he could catch a glimpse of Blue tiptoeing through the forest?

But the massive trees were shielding his view and the only sounds in this land of frozen silence were those of his own footsteps.

"Blue?!" called the dog once more, wishing for an answer more than anything else.

Only the crunching of his paws on the frozen snow filled the air, there was no other sound to give away his friend's whereabouts.

In vain the dog tried to obtain an answer from Blue. He called and called, his eyes searching the dark woods while his paws struggled to stay close to the patch of light pouring from his burrow.

"Crunch-crunch", the snow answered from beneath his feet.

What a long time of searching that had been!

Reaching the door again, with his head low and his tail tucked between his hind legs, Little Tail sighed.

"Blue will return again when he wants to play... I hope."

Then, as a new thought sprang into Little Tail's mind, the dog seemed to brighten up a little. With head held high once more, eyes filled with excitement and one front paw pointing, up went a corner of his mouth.

"Tea!"

It wasn't a discovery, rather a conclusion. A very pleasant one indeed.

And soon both corners of his mouth pulled up into a smile.

"I'll setup my observation point again... with a cup of tea!"

His smile was wider now, as he licked his snout. For the desire had become a necessity and, in time, the necessity had turned into a habit: "and something to munch on, of course!"

His tongue performed another wiping motion over his lips.

"I'll be sure to catch a glimpse of Blue, sooner or later. We had so much good fun last night! But until then..." and his eyebrows quickly rose and lowered themselves, finishing off the tasty thought.

A few moments later, with a steaming cup of tea in his paws, the dog had nestled himself once more on his little stool by the window.

"Ahhh!" he smiled while closing his eyes dreamily, sniffing at the refreshing aroma rising from his nutshell.

"Nothing like a good-old cup of fir tea", he muttered while gazing admiringly at the bright green liquid. Then, facing the window, he began to wait for Blue.

It was but an instant later that he jumped off his seat.

"Wait a minute, what's this?"

Little Tail cocked his head.

A blurred picture formed in front of his eyes, with the trees outlined against the whiteness of the Snow. Everything else was blurred by clouds.

"How could the clouds descend so low?" The dog was puzzled.

He placed his face even closer to the window, hoping for a better picture. But his long snout was in the way and it touched the cold window-pane.

"Ha-chu!" he sneezed and his whole

body shook.

One sip of tea later, Little Tail tried to focus his eyes onto the window again.

Same blurry, cloudy picture... except for a little spot where...

"Hello, what's this?" the dog's eyebrows lifted themselves in wonder.

On the window pane, right in the middle of the blurry image, there was now a clear spot!

Little Tail carefully placed his left eye against it. And this one eye saw a perfect picture forming outside, in which the trees were neatly outlined and no clouds were floating above the ground.

The dog blinked and shook his head in disbelief. He now opened his right eye too, but his right eye was seeing the old, blurry image!

"How can this be?! My left eye sees

something, while my right eye sees something else?"

Shifting his head he placed his right eye against the miraculous spot. He watched closely and...

"Brrr!" he pulled right back as his cheek had accidently touched something icy. Wiping the cold droplets off his fur Little Tail faced the window again and...

How marvellous and how strange!

Now both his eyes could see a clear picture at the same time!

And both his eyes saw...

"Blue!!"

Blue was outside, seated on the very same spot he had occupied earlier in the evening.

The two friends waved at each other, both of them just as excited.

A thrill of delight went all throughout Little Tail's body, starting at the very tip of his snout and ending with the red tuft of his tail. And almost instantly a broad smile lit up his whole face.

"Come in!" gestured Little Tail while lifting his nut shell in an invitation to share a cup of tea.

"Ooo!" he exclaimed the very next moment. Because, to his utmost surprise, Blue was also grasping a nutshell, matching the one Little Tail was holding.

"Ooo!" the dog hardly believed his eyes for his friend had just sipped from his cup, at exactly the same moment he had drank from his own!

So that's why Blue disappeared, to fetch a cup of tea!

"Oh, Blue, my friend", Little Tail

shook his head, "you could have asked ME for tea!"

And Blue shook his head too as if in reply: "no, I dared not", then took another sip.

In the blink of an eye Little Tail had opened his front door and leaped outside. His ears were waving up and down in the rhythm of his paws which were bouncing excitedly on the frozen snow, his tail faithfully wagging behind.

"Let's play!" he called out, running towards his friend.

Little Tail's tongue was hanging loose, his mouth open in the widest smile possible.

Not seeing his friend at first, the dog bounced a few steps left, stopping short, then bounced a few steps right. He bounced left again, right again, left, right, his leaps becoming shorter and less vigorous with every hop.

Until he suddenly stopped.

"Blue?!!" he called out in disbelief, for once again his friend was gone!

"Not again!" exclaimed his heart.

Was he perhaps looking for Blue in the wrong place? A little hope made its way inside Little Tail's mind. His eyes feverishly searched the ground around him.

Here, behind him, was his window. And here, in front of him, was the log of wood on which Blue had been sitting only moments ago!

Little Tail sniffed the surrounding air, trying to catch Blue's scent. He could feel his heart pounding in his chest, beating loudly. Could Blue hear it too?

The dog took two steps to the right, then two steps to the left. Something crackled behind him. He spun on his heels.

"It must be Blue; it has to be Blue..." he whispered to himself, his tail suddenly very close to his body. "I hope it's Blue... Blue was just here before. Could he be hiding? Oh!" and the thought made his eyes shine. Even his tail wagged a little.

"So this is it! A game of hide-and-seek!"

"All right, Blue!" called out Little Tail, braving himself. "You're it! Ready or not, here I come..." and with a loud, energized bark he began his hunt.

He ran towards the nearest tree, stopping short then rapidly searching behind it... nothing. But out of the corner of his eye he caught a glimpse of movement behind a nearby heap of snow. Sure of himself he ran towards it and, with a sudden jump...

"Found you!"

Only to discover that he was wrong. Not one sign of Blue, not even a footprint!

For a long time the little dog ran around, searching for his friend. Again and again he pounced on heaps of snow and jumped behind shrubs, sure to have spotted Blue hiding there. But Blue was nowhere to be found.

His snout soon began to freeze in the icy air.

Panting, exhausted and deeply saddened Little Tail found himself outside his burrow again. His head was hanging low, a little wrinkle of skin forming along his snout, his ears almost touching the ice-covered earth and his tail, having lost its bounce altogether, plummeted to the ground.

He would have sat to catch his breath, once he did try to sit, but the snow made his fur wet, chilling him to the bone.

So he just stood there on his short, exhausted feet, right outside his door, feeling that he could easily sink into the ground with sadness. His heart had certainly dropped into his chest.

"Blue, I give up now!" he called one last time. Then, almost in a whisper: "you win."

Lifting one small eyebrow, throwing one last glance around, ever so slowly he turned his back to the forest, heading for home.

What happened next could have

been the result of the prolonged time Little Tail had spent outside, in the cold, snowy night. Or perhaps of the fact that his snout had been too close to the icy ground for too long. Or maybe, just maybe, his clever nose had indeed caught a faint scent of Blue and, as every dog's snout would have done, had sent a signal to his owner.

Like a smoke signal.

What's certain is that Little Tail sneezed.

"Achoo!"

His ears flapped.

"Achoo!"

His front paws bounced off the ground.

"Sniff, sniff."

He tried to scratch his nose but it

tickled on the inside!

"A – A – ACHOO!"

His whole body shook and it shot backwards. His stout behind hit a nearby tree.

"Thump!"

And before Little Tail could even excuse himself a heap of snow fell, "splat!" right... next to him.

Had the pile of snow been covering the moonlight all along? Or had the moon itself parted the clouds to have a better look at the lonely dog? What is sure is that, after Little Tail had picked himself up and shook himself a little, starting with his head and finishing off with the tuft of red fur at the very end of his tail, when he looked around... a sea of blue shadows seemed to have emerged from behind every single tree, every single snow heap, no matter how small.

The half circle of light cast onto the Snow by his open door looked less bright now as up in the sky the moon came out.

Little Tail felt cold... very cold, lonely and quite lost without his friend. And a little bit scared too.

He had searched and searched, called out loud and even whispered softly, he had written his friend's name in the Snow, howled it out in sorrow...

Still, Blue had neither answered, nor shown up.

With his tail between his legs, the dog dragged his little feet back towards his burrow.

His tea would have long gone cold... well, at least his bed was there and he could pile the leaves on top of himself, warm up his frozen paws and his icy cold tail... and his freezing ears... and his chilled body and...

Half-turned towards the forest he threw one last glimpse behind. Even the trees had company now, their own shadows.

He glanced up towards the bright moon.

"Who had put it there? Whose doorlight was it, shining in the night? Did it belong to a house? A house in the sky? Whose path did it light?"

With his eyes filled by the light of the moon Little Tail almost, almost missed seeing Blue!

For his friend was suddenly there, sitting close by and as quiet as ever, watching the bright circle above...

"Blue?!" whispered Little Tail, not sure if he should believe his eyes or not. "You're here? You're here!"

And Blue ran towards Little Tail at precisely the same moment Little Tail rushed towards Blue.

"So that light, up there, is yours? Is it?" the dog shook his head and Blue nodded his answer back, in agreement.

"Is the light from your home? Oh, silly, silly me, now I understand! But where have you been sitting? Where have you been hiding? Have you not heard me calling for you? Have you not..." and Little Tail poured a bucket of questions over Blue while, at the same time, rising his paws in question.

And Blue raised his paws too and shuddered, just as Little Tail did.

"Oh, oh, oh", exclaimed the dog,

"does it really matter now? Let's PLAY! Yippee! That's a sure thing!" concluded an exhausted, but extremely happy dog.

And just as happy, Blue agreed.

CHAPTER 8

THE SECRET OF THE OLD, BENDY TREE

Secrets like to hibernate. Therefore they will only consent to their discovery at a specific moment in time, when the world, or yourself, are ready for them.

For secrets like to stay hidden, they like to ripen first. Most like a bread which first has to be kneaded, allowed time to rise, baked afterwards and oh, then, then one still has to wait for it to cool down before one can enjoy it.

Finally!

But when the moment is just right the most wonderful secrets can be revealed to you and then, only then will you come to understand that your previous actions have quietly been preparing you for this moment all alone.

Or so says The Book of Life.

"Tweet-tweet..."

"Tweet-tweet..."

Little Tail turned over in his bed, squeezed his eyes tight and pulled the leaf-blanket over his head.

"Tweet-tweet!"

"Tweet-tweet!"

"Hmm..." moaned the dog, half asleep. His body felt warm and cosy in his leafy bed, not in the least ready to wake up. But his mind decided it had slept enough. Little Tail's brain was awake, intrigued by the noise outside in spite of his body still enjoying its comfy surroundings.

"It can't be Blue. Blue doesn't tweet. Blue doesn't make any sound at all", thought the dog while cautiously peeping from under his quilt.

"Tweet-tweet!!"

The noise was louder and clearer now, coming from just outside his window.

"Maybe if I don't move at all it will think there is no-one here... and it will go away", Little Tail tried to lie still under his blanky.

But the noise wouldn't conform. Clearly, whoever was creating the noise had a good enough reason for it. And it wasn't only to wake up the sleepy occupant of this cosy, homely burrow.

"Tweet-tweet!"

"Knock-knock!"

"Tweet-tweet!"

"And now? It knocks on my window too! I wonder if it's important... or just impatient."

Little Tail lifted his leafy quilt a little bit more, taking a further look at his window.

At first, fresh from under the darkness of his covers, he only saw a blur of light. He blinked and blinked some more. Now he could clearly see the window.

The sun was shining brightly and joyful rays were pouring inside his burrow. How happy the sun was!

"Sunny Day!" Little Tail's heart sang.

"It must have been up for a long time", observed the dog, wondering about the time of day. Judging by the gurgling sounds made by his tummy it was well past breakfast.

The tweeting and knocking seemed to have stopped and everything was quiet again.

Lost in hungry thoughts Little Tail pondered, "Should I have a quick snack before breakfast or will this spoil my appetite?"

He didn't notice the silhouette outside. But when the next "tweet-

tweet" was followed by a "rat-tat-tat" knocking on the door, his room was already darkened by a shadow covering most of his window.

"Ooo..." Little Tail's voice trembled now, "who could be so b-b-big and b-b-be looking for me?"

Breakfast plans suddenly forgotten the dog made himself as small as he possibly could underneath his leafy beddings.

Will the shadow appear smaller if he took just a little peek at it?

It worked! There seemed to be less of a shadow now looming outside his window. Summoning up his courage he took a better look and saw a...

"Bird!" he exclaimed, relieved, recognising the source of noise for what it really was.

"A tiny birdie! Aww!" cooed the dog as he jumped out of bed and took one step towards the window.

For the window was only two steps away from his bed.

A little smile curled up the corners of Little Tail's mouth.

How he would like to play with Bird! Birds could also talk! In tweeted words, but he would have someone to chat to, someone that would also answer, for a change...

Even though he had so much fun playing with Blue, Little Tail missed listening to another voice. He longed to hear the beautiful succession of sounds and pauses that builds itself into a mosaic of questions and answers. The kind that two friends would weave together when carrying a conversation.

Blue was fun to play with. Blue was a great race partner, especially when running around his burrow! Blue could jump almost as high as he did. Yes, Blue was a great match during play time. But Little Tail longed to talk to someone. To be obliged to remain quiet, in turns, while that someone would answer him.

He never imagined he would miss the   I-talk-then-I-listen-while-you-talk game! But he did so, terribly!

Hopefully, he glanced again towards the window, but the bird was nowhere to be seen... or heard. There was nothing out there but the bright sunshine, the snow and the silence.

You might think that the dog just stood there, in the middle of his tiny room, feeling lonely and gloomy.

Well, he did stand there for a little while, maybe for as long as it took him to realise that Bird was gone... or perhaps a few seconds longer. But then another noise came through and Little Tail knew he simply had to do something about it!

For his tummy was growling again, producing louder and louder noises, each one more urgent. Little Tail disliked the sounds of his hungry stomach and he most definitely did not enjoy the feeling of it.

So he spun around, grabbed a bowl, one of those nut shell bowls he had carved for himself, put some food in it and began to prepare an aromatic, hot cup of fir tea to wash it down with.

"Right", whispered Little Tail looking a bit confused. Something seemed to be missing from his tiny pantry...

"But what?"

Something very important, of course... Something he needed now... Something for his tea, perhaps?

He had his tiny kettle, the fire was on, there were more than enough fir leaves ... still, something was missing.

"Ah, ha!" he exclaimed, pointing up a finger. "Water! Water was the missing ingredient!"

For there was no water left in his little room. All the water supply had been used up last night when he'd been sipping his tea, cup after cup, while waiting for Blue to appear.

"Oh, well, if water is needed, then I better go get some!" And as quick as you could say "water" he collected his scarf, his teapot, an extra nut shell and was already outside in search of fresh, clean snow.

For what else would you use as a

source of water in such a snowy place?

A picture in white, sparkling brightly and cheerfully, met his eyes the instant he opened the door.

The sun was shining over the snow covered forest and the day was even brighter than yesterday!

At least that's what Little Tail thought.

Cheered up by the sun, for he loved

a sunny day, Little Tail danced a happy jig outside his door before going in search of clean snow.

"Tweet-tweet!"

From up in a tree.

"Tweet-tweet!"

Being careful not to scare Bird again, the dog slowly lifted his head towards the source of the noise, peaking at a branch just above his window.

Of course, he would not have seen the bird perched so high up when he looked from inside his burrow, for she was seated right above his roof!

"She hasn't flown away after all! She's just perched up there, waiting."

Little Tail smiled to himself. It was good to know he hadn't scared Bird away!

The dog was now contemplating the idea of having someone as chatty as Bird living just outside his home. Someone to talk to during the day... Oh, he would like that very much!

But now it was breakfast time and the roaring of his tummy didn't allow for chit-chats.

"Sorry, Bird, I just have to get some water for my breakfast."

To his surprise and joy the bird flew down, landing on a heap of snow just a few steps away from him. She considered him with a curious eye, glistening like a star in the night, her black head tilted to one side. Then she turned her head the other side, watching Little Tail with her other eye. Finally she spun around and, with teeny hops, she skipped towards a knobbly tree nearby.

Hop-hop, bounced her little body.

Up and down, up and down swished her long tail. And her feet left distinctive marks on the fresh snow.

"Like a forked branch", thought the dog.

Only then he saw it, behind the bird, the tree.

Little Tail knew that tree very well. He had noticed it the day he arrived here, an old, twisted tree full of knots and hollows. But it had frightened him then and it still made him nervous now, in the bright, cheerful morning.

"Bird, you're brave, but I will not follow you now, not to the knobbly tree anyway…"

He busied himself with his nutshell. "I have to collect snow for my water, have my breakfast and then we can chat… somewhere else, perhaps?"

And on saying so, Little Tail turned towards the opposite direction, ready to collect fresh snow. For fresh snow was everywhere in sight!

But the bird would have none of it! Flying back onto her branch she tweet-tweet-ed towards Little Tail, flew down again, watching him, tilting her tiny head sideways, only to hop again towards the knobbly tree.

"Uh, oh?" murmured Little Tail to himself, watching the bird out of the corner of his eye. "What could this mean?"

And he prepared again to fill up his nut shell with fresh snow.

The bird performed her strange routine once again, then flew back to perch herself on her branch, above Little Tail's burrow.

A narrow pathway leading to the old, knobbly tree had been laid down by the bird's hopping of to and fro. The dog looked uncertainly at it.

"Interesting", thought Little Tail,

taking only one step onto the freshly laid path.

"Tweet-Tweet! Tweet-Tweet!" the bird chirped loud and clear from her branch.

The dog glanced at her over his shoulder.

The intelligent bird was watching him, dancing on her branch. Suddenly she flew past him, barely touching the top of his head with her wing, landing on the freshly laid path and, after one last hop, she perched herself onto a low branch of the old tree....

Then, tweeting once more she flew away!

Gone!

"Bird!" called out Little Tail, "Wait!" He barked out loud and his nose twitched. But the bird was nowhere in sight.

The dog glanced towards the old tree. His tail drew closer to his body.

"I wonder..." he whispered to himself as he placed his pails full of snow down. "I just wonder..." he murmured once more, a little bit louder this time as the sound of his own voice helped him summon his courage. "What was Bird trying to tell me? Why did she bother to lay down this path?"

His nose twitched again. His eyebrows rose as he measured the bendy tree.

Was there something hidden in there, for him to discover?

What could it be?

A message?

A treasure?

The thought of a mystery just waiting to be solved gave Little Tail an extra boost of courage. Now that he was feeling a little braver he slowly started to walk along the trail, towards the old tree.

Taking small steps, his tail lowered

cautiously while his eyes kept the target in sight, he approached the knobbly tree. His eyes watching it, studying it, his body ready to jump off the track and run home if any strange movement occurred. He took one step and then another and one more... It seemed to take forever to walk along the short path.

Eventually the bird trail was finished and he was standing, at last, in front of the old, bendy tree.

Little Tail slowly lifted his head, measuring the tree from bottom to top. Standing so close the old arbour seemed even more impressive as it towered over the small dog.

It was gigantic.

"Oooh", whispered Little Tail and steam came out of his mouth for it was shady there, near the old tree, and the morning air was cold.

Little Tail turned his head, curious about the steam dispersing all around him. He blew more hot air. It made another tiny cloud of fog which also dissolved around Little Tail. The dog lifted his front paw and blew over it. For a second his paw disappeared out of view, covered by the cloud of steam produced by his mouth. Little Tail gave a little laugh.

How funny that was, he could make parts of himself disappear!

But no echo answered his laugh and when the last bit of fog was gone the old, knobbly tree was standing in front of him again.

Little Tail knew he had to continue his search. He'd come so far along the bird's trail, he had to find out what needed to be discovered by someone such as himself, a little dog. The thought that someone as small as him was expected to unravel this mystery made his heart beat faster, making him feel excited and scared at the same time.

He looked up again. The tree seemed to expand over him, the branches covering the sky above his head. For a moment Little Tail felt all his courage disappearing, evaporating around him like the fog he had just blown.

"What now?"

The only noise the dog could hear was the pounding of his own heart.

"Little beings can also do great things!" a thought surfaced.

Where did that come from? Yes, that's right, he had read it in The Book of Life.

With this belief in mind he held himself taller and began walking slowly, making his way around the thick trunk, studying it the way a warrior would study his opponent before a battle.

But Little Tail was a small dog and the ancient tree was large and very knobbly so this confrontation wouldn't have been a fair one at all.

Only the arbour did not seem to look for a quarrel at all, on the contrary. It just stood there, towering over the forest with its height and vast amount of branches which appeared to grow in every direction. He just stood there, allowing the small creature to study him.

It took Little Tail a long time to walk all around the enormous trunk.

"Nothing, nothing at all", he murmured on reaching the bird trail again.

He had walked all around the gigantic tree without finding anything unusual about it. It was just a tree.

Little Tail's courage rose and he felt in good spirits once again.

"What can be so special about you?" he spoke, tilting his head to one shoulder, narrowing his eyes and giving the tree one last scrutinising look.

What happened next can be looked at as a mere coincidence or, perhaps, it had been Bird's doing again, flying over Little Tail's head once more and producing a drift of air…

The undeniable fact is that a pile of snow fell from the knobbly tree at precisely this moment to reveal a hollow right above the ground, exactly in front of Little Tail!

"Ooo", gasped the small dog.

This revelation was more than he had expected. For a long minute he felt at a loss for words.

"Ooo", was all he could exclaim. Finally, he whispered in amazement, as if to advise himself to keep this discovery a secret: "a tree hollow!"

And then Little Tail smiled.

Tree hollows were something very dear to his heart as he often made his home inside them. Drawing from his long experience he could definitely confirm that tree hollows were bearers of wonderful surprises. Because having been inhabited by so many animals in turn, whenever one moved out several goodies were often left behind. As a token of consideration towards the next tenant, of course.

How wonderful was that! It was a very, very pleasing thought indeed.

In the late winter morning, standing in front of the newly discovered hollow with the noise of his rumbling tummy still echoing in his ears, Little Tail's eyes were sparkling with anticipation.

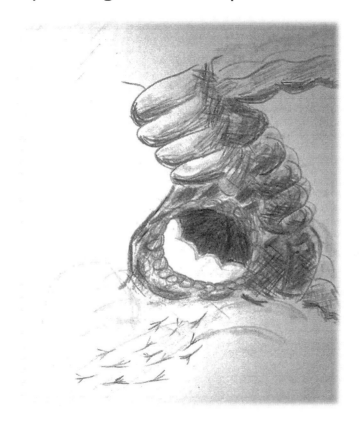

Soon enough his curiosity got the better of him and, leaving any trace of shyness behind, he stepped forward to have a peek inside this treasure chest that had suddenly opened up in front of him.

At a first glance the dog felt rather disappointed as he found nothing of value, just a pile of dry leaves. It was only after he looked around for a second time that he caught a glimpse of green shimmering underneath the foliage.

"Hmm?" the dog raised an eyebrow. Not many types of food stay green this late in winter.

"What am I saying? No food stays fresh and green halfway through winter!" he exclaimed out loud in order to cover the growling noises made by his stomach.

It must have been the gush of air which came out of his mouth as he spoke that blew the dry leaves apart. For the morning air was as still and as bright as it was frozen, not the slightest breeze could be felt throughout the whole forest.

And so, he saw it.

Lying on the burrow's floor, underneath the thick layer of leaves.

"Could this really be...?"

CHAPTER 9

LITTLE TAIL AND DRAGONFLY

Sometimes, as we happen upon life's winding paths in search of a goal or perhaps following our dreams, we have no other choice but to leave friends behind. If this happens don't despair for just when you believe that you will be all alone, for a long, long time, new friends will come your way.

Such are the joys of life, because friendship gives life meaning and our hearts, knowing this, are constantly searching for those special companions.

Or so says The Book of Life.

And then Little Tail saw it...

It had been lying there all along, hidden underneath the thick layer of dry leaves, part hibernating, perhaps even unconscious, but for how long?

"Covered by the leaves or covered with the leaves?" murmured the dog, "and by whom?"

"Bird..." he answered softly, throwing a glance outside. Only now did he understand Bird's clever plan. The tweeting, the knocking, the path she had laid...

His eyes swept over the bare, dark walls of the tree hollow and rested again on the shape lying at his feet.

Right there, on the very bottom of this seemingly deserted burrow, between dry leaves spread all around, lay a dragonfly!

"Sleepy? Frozen?... Dead...?" He gave a little shiver. "Surely not, I hope not!" whispered Little Tail and his bottom lip trembled.

"Catch a dragonfly and it will chase you away,

Save a dragonfly and you will soon be on your way."

And the words nearly spoke themselves, for the dog didn't even realize that he had hummed the old chant.

"What should I do, what should I do?" Little Tail whispered, fidgeting, for the old rhyme he used to sing back in his beloved Woodland now made him question how truthful it really was.

"Catch a dragonfly and it will chase you away,

Save a dragonfly and you will soon be on your way."

But nobody he knew had ever caught one, let alone saved one...

Dragonflies were known for darting above waters in solitary flights. Nobody made friends with such creatures! At least nobody he or his friends back home had ever heard of... They all just sang the old tune whenever they spotted one. They just did it.

Out of habit? Superstition? They never paused to question it.

Until now...

"Well, since she's just lying here it won't mean that I've caught her if I carry her into my burrow to warm her up... will it?"

Trying to be as quiet as possible he inspected the lifeless insect. "Hopefully it will mean that I've saved you", he added wishfully for he really did not want to be chased away from his cosy little home. And definitely not in the heart of winter!

Yes, saving the frozen insect seemed the right thing to do. And he nodded in agreement, giving himself courage.

He set to work as quickly as he could.

First he covered the dragonfly again to keep her warm while he rushed to his burrow to return the water pails, stir the fire and put the kettle on for tea.

He also searched for the biggest leaf-duvet he owned. He would need it to transport the dragonfly, from the hollow to his burrow.

But this last task proved easier said than done as, to transport the dragonfly, what a challenge! Carefully folding the insect's enormous wings the dog, ever so slowly, rolled her onto the leaf. Then, tying a long string of grass all around this gigantic parcel, he swung the other end over a low branch outside, creating a pulley to ease his load. Slowly, carefully, by pulling on the loose end of grass, he lifted the frozen body out of the opening of the tree hollow and, finally, slid it along the snowy path and into his own burrow.

Giving a sigh of relief the dog smiled to himself self-assured. He was now inside his cosy, little home... all alone... with the frozen dragonfly.

"Catch a dragonfly and it will chase you away,

Save a dragonfly and you will soon be on your way."

Little Tail looked down at the motionless insect now lying on his bed.

"This bed is just the right size for you... Please don't chase me away when you wake up", he pleaded then he sniffed cautiously towards the guest. No change.

So he set to work, doing what should be done, helping, and pushing future worries out of his mind. At least for now.

He will have to gradually warm up the frozen body in order to safely wake the dragonfly from her frozen sleep.

"But before I do this, I really, really need to have some hot tea and a bite or two... or maybe three to eat!"

His stomach agreed with a growl,

Little Tail tried in vain to silence it.

The evening had soon settled and Little Tail was still doing his best to warm up the frozen insect.

He had been working the entire day heating up chestnuts and placing them strategically around the icy body.

He had covered the insect with two of his best dry leaf blankets.

The fire was burning steadily in his tiny fireplace and the tea was being kept just warm enough, as to not burn the poor patient. Although he felt tired himself, Little Tail's spirits were high as he could now see that his efforts were slowly being rewarded: the insect's body was slowly warming up.

"Poor damsel", murmured the dog throwing a compassionate look towards his patient. "You poor soul, what a terrible experience to freeze like that."

Then he dutifully felt the chestnuts placed around the dragonfly, found one that needed reheating and set himself to work, by the stove, absorbed by the task at hand.

A soft flutter stirred the Dragonfly's wings. Still, they remained folded.

Warming up a chestnut is no child's play. One has to be careful not to burn oneself and, of course, not to overheat the nut either.

The leaves covering the patient roused a little and the dragonfly's enormous eyes stirred underneath her closed eyelids.

The chestnut had to be just warm enough, not cooked; Little Tail remembered his mother's advice. Careful not to burn himself, the dog picked up the hot nut with the aid of a leaf and approached his patient again.

"Gently does it", he murmured to himself then he noticed the fallen bed covers. "How silly to have tumbled like this."

He was just about to fix them when he stopped, his arm suspended in mid-air. The covers would not have moved by themselves... unless... unless...

His tail suddenly ducked between his legs.

"Oopsy daisy", whispered the little dog, worried by the sudden change in situation. "Oh, dear me, I truly hope you're a peaceful soul. I worked so hard to bring you back to life, please be a kind dragonfly..."

"Dragonflies are always kind", the answer came in a low murmur.

Little Tail's chin dropped. His tongue fell out. His plump behind ducked a little too, following his tail.

He was not prepared for a talking dragonfly. Of course, this is what he'd been hoping for, for the insect to come back to life. But it happened too quickly! Shouldn't a frozen body take longer to warm up? Perhaps… days?

"Of course, of course", the dog tried to brace himself, "of course it had to come back to life… eventually. But so soon…Oh dear, what am I supposed to do now? Look at me…I'm so scared, I sweat! Oh, she will see I'm scared, oh, what if she will chase me away?"

The fear had the small dog frozen in his tracks, right by the bed from which the awoken patient was watching him.

The dragonfly, her eyes now wide open, was observing the funny little creature standing next to her, covered in sweat while holding a hot nut in his fiddling paws.

"Dragonflies are always kind", she repeated in a gentle, low voice. Then she added with a smile. "Do you enjoy being so hot? You have a cosy place here and I am a thousand times grateful to you for saving me and bringing me back to life. But that heated nut is making you sweat, my friend."

Little Tail was staring in disbelief at the talking insect he had rescued.

How clearly she spoke and how sweet her voice was! How pleasant it was to hear someone else addressing him in plain words, so agreeable, like music to his ears.

"A singing Dragonfly!" he exclaimed out loud, without even realising that he was no longer talking to only himself.

The insect blinked in agreement and when she opened her eyes again they seemed even bigger. She laughed softly.

"You're a funny little creature... a thousand thanks again for saving me..."

"My pleasure! One can't leave another soul to die", smiled Little Tail feeling very much like a hero.

His heartbeat had slowed down and, upon hearing the insect's friendly voice, he felt... almost safe enough to come nearer and place the hot chestnut back in its place.

Almost, but not quite.

Instead, he straightened himself and, while still holding the heated nut, he introduced himself.

"I am a dog. My name is Little Tail."

"So pleased to meet you. I am Dragonfly and I never thought I'd see the light of day again... or feel the warmth of the sun on my wings... or in this case of a heated chestnut."

And she gave a little laugh, half closing her eyes, to show how happy she really was to be alive. Then her eyelids closed altogether.

Little Tail jumped at the chance and replaced the nutshell by his patient.

He felt braver when the insect kept still and quiet and her enormous eyes were closed.

Then Dragonfly started speaking

again.

"I hurt my wing and, while waiting for it to get better, the frost came. It arrived too early this year", she gave a little shiver.

"So it caught me outside my wintery hole, away from my family and friends. Then the Snow fell and I was trapped in that hollow where you found me... But how did you?"

The insect opened her eyes again and Little Tail could see how big and beautiful they really were and how friendly they smiled at him.

He felt more at ease than he'd ever been since he'd found her.

"Oh", sighed the insect, "thank you, I still feel like I need all the heat I can get. Your hot nutshells are most welcome indeed. How did you find me?

Has the Snow melted already?"

Little Tail coughed, feeling a little embarrassed, as he always was every time he had to talk about himself.

"Well, Bird showed me where to search. I found you in the tree hollow. Pardon me, but you looked frozen to death. I brought you here, warmed you up and, luckily, you came back to life!" Then he coughed again and quickly changed the subject.

"Would you like a cup of tea, perhaps?"

"I have freshly made tea, spicy and hot, fir leaves boiled in snow water, sunny-snow. I personally don't like the shady snow for making tea. Do you? The sunny-snow gives the tea a delicate flavour."

And while chatting away, Little Tail

came back holding two nutshells of perfectly brewed tea; one for the patient, one for himself.

"Try some, it will do you a world of good", he handed one cup over with a smile, a big smile.

Dragonfly slowly propped herself upright, her wings still closed around her body. Her saviour's tiny burrow would not have been spacious enough for her wings to unfold wide open! She took sip of tea to be polite.

Dragonflies don't normally drink tea. They live during hot summer months so they have no need for hot cups of sunny-snow tea.

Dragonflies like darting in cool waters and breezy winds which carry them flying far and away.

Dragonflies are brave and

adventurous. They take to the air in an instant and are out of your eye sight in a flash, always on the lookout for the next cool splash of water or swift air-stream.

But this Dragonfly lying in Little Tail's burrow had been terribly sick, even worse, almost frozen to death and only just brought back to life by a miracle with four paws and a tail. So this Dragonfly took a sip of sunny-snow hot tea and, believe it or not, she liked it!

"Very good indeed!" she smiled towards her friendly saviour, a tired smile. "Best tea I ever drank", she nodded as she closed her eyes and her cheeks kept their pallor.

No blood rose to paint them with the liar's red, for she was telling the truth.

"I love sunny-snow tea, reminds me of my home forest... although we don't have snow back home..." replied the dog with a deep sigh.

"Is this not your home then?" Dragonfly had stirred from her slumber. She blinked a few times and looked around in surprise, taking in the pleasant room.

Seeing it for the first time as it really was, well-furnished and filled with anything your heart desired for a warm and comfy living, although all the objects surrounding her were brand new, she noticed now.

Little Tail fidgeted on his little chair. After taking another sip of tea he began telling his story about his beloved Woodland with its pleasant weather, big lake and shady trees, about his dear friends and about his irresistible desire to see the Snow. Which had brought him here.

Dragonfly showed great interest in the dog's story and her wings had stirred a little when the big, shady lake was mentioned.

"Then why don't you go back home if you miss your friends this much? You have met the Snow... and turned into a Snowdog", her mouth stretched in a smile. "Even if only for one night... Of course, your friend Blue might miss you after you're gone. But if he's half as pleasant as you say, he's bound to make new friends soon, despite his shyness."

"You know", Little Tail whispered while looking into his cup, "I think Blue might have been my own shadow..."

And he paused feeling uncomfortable to confess that he had an imaginary friend.

Dragonfly nodded. Slowly, she placed an arm over the dog's paw.

Sometimes words are not needed to make ourselves understood.

The dog gave a sigh of relief and went on.

"You see, against the whiteness of the Snow the night's shadows are so blue up here."

Beaming with the excitement of his discovery he went on.

"I never thought of it this way, but the shadows back home are rather... green!" He eagerly explained himself. "Because of our Woodland, with its green leaves. You see, there are so many lovely green trees in my home forest!"

"And a lake", smiled Dragonfly dreamily.

"And a lake", confirmed the dog with a sigh. "While here", and he pointed outside, "here everything is white... or blue! Or blue and white. Neither green, nor gold, nor yellow", he paused for breath then went on, with eyes half closed, describing a picture he knew so well and held in his heart. "No dotted reds, nor floral violets, no sunny greens, nor shady teals... no sundown orange, nor sunrise pinks. And definitely no ice-cream clouds!"

"So", questioned Dragonfly as dragonflies do tend to be persistent and she, too, knew a thing or two about colours. Not so much though about... ice-cream clouds?

"Why don't you go back home then?"

"Oh..." sighed Little Tail even deeper and his shoulders dropped. "Ooooh", he gave out a little sob and he looked so miserable that Dragonfly felt sorry for being so nosey.

The dog fiddled with his nutshell.

"I wanted to see the Snow, yes, but now the only thing that brought me here also keeps me in this place. For the Snow has covered the pathway I arrived on. Everything looks different now, yet, wherever I gaze everything looks the same. So white and sparkly, yet the same. I won't be able to find my way back home. And the Snow is so fluffy and deep. I might sink in at any step and freeze to death."

Here the dog coughed a bit, suddenly realizing that this subject might be a sensitive one for Dragonfly. But the insect was keeping quiet and her eyelids were half closed, dreamily.

"So you see", whispered Little Tail, "I have to wait until the Snow melts…" He sighed. "If Snow will ever melt in this icy land!"

Little Tail's ears fell forward and a small tear rolled down his cheek. With a silent splash it fell inside his cup of sunny-snow tea. He looked so small and sorrowful sitting on his little chair that Dragonfly wished she could hug him. But she was still too weak.

"Even his own tears feel sorry for him", she thought. "Oh, he's such a caring little dog, he saved my life and what do I do in return? I make him cry!"

"There, there", the insect tried to comfort her small saviour. "I'm sure we can find a solution to your problem. If we think smart enough then we shall find it."

And having just said this, as if by magic or perhaps through her desire to help a friend in need, an idea sparked into Dragonfly's mind.

"What am I talking about?!" she

exclaimed filled with joyous excitement. "If you cannot walk back home, then you shall fly there!"

Little Tail was so surprised by the unexpected solution that, for a moment, he forgot all about his sadness, too curious to find out what Dragonfly was talking about.

"Fly?" he repeated, not believing his ears. "Me? Fly? Fly all the way back to my Woodland home? But how? I may be small, but I'm still a dog and my homeland lies far, far away. I can't even recall how many days it took me to get here…"

"I shall fly you there!" declared Dragonfly and her front legs moved in a swift, flying movement.

"Catch a dragonfly and it will chase you away,

Save a dragonfly and you can soon be on your way."

whispered Little Tail.

Dragonfly narrowed her eyes, "hmm-mm, not true at all! Not the first part, anyway. Someone must have said it to make us look scary... I wonder who and why?"

And Dragonfly was deep in thought for a few seconds.

Little Tail watched her in sheer wonder. His eyes wide open, filled with excitement, his mouth just as wide, his tongue hanging. He wasn't sure what he found more astonishing.

The fact that the dragonfly he saved had just offered to fly him back home... or the fact that the ancient rhyme was true... except for the first part, of course. He could feel his heart pounding in his chest and he wished he could sing and dance with joy. But he felt shy to do so in front of his new friend. He could only wait, bursting with excitement.

"So you also know it, the rhyme? I've known it ever since I can remember!"

"Know it?!" boomed Dragonfly. "But of course I do, it is part of our vow", she proclaimed.

Then added in a more subdued tone, "and it isn't a rhyme, my friend. Don't call it such as it is much more solemn. It is a Code of Honour." And to emphasize its importance she crossed her right front leg over her chest, pushed up her chin and, eyelids half closed, cited:

"Catch a dragonfly and it will fight you right away,

Save a dragonfly and you can

soon be on your way."

Silence covered the burrow.

"I'll fly you back to your Woodland home!" promised the insect solemnly as to seal the deal.

CHAPTER 10

SOMETHING EXTRAORDINARY HAPPENS

A promise is a promise and it has to be honoured. But if help is required in order to fulfil it, then help must be asked for. And if help is being asked for, then help must be provided.

One must always offer one's help when friends or well-being are concerned.

Or so says The Book of Life.

Early one morning, just as Little Tail woke up and was still stretching his toes under the duvet, his gaze went, as always, to the window. He had learned to predict the extent of the day's snow by the darkness of the daybreak clouds.

But this morning his heart almost jumped out of his chest at the sight that met his eyes. The corners of his mouth pulled back into a broad smile and in an instant he was by the window.

Was it for real?

Did it really happen?

Yes it was!

Yes it did!

And his tail agreed too.

Not being able to contain himself, he stirred the fire out of habit then went back to sit on his bed. He gazed outside again. He rubbed his eyes. He ran to the window, this time looking up, up towards the sky.

It **WAS** a bright, sunny morning!

"**TODAY** is the day!"

"Today **IS** the day!"

"**THE** day is today!"

"I'm flying home today... back to my Woodland!" he hummed to himself smiling broadly while doing his morning exercises. And his heart smiled too, he felt it smiling inside his chest.

Just a few days earlier Dragonfly had

advised him on the best conditions for their departure together: right after breakfast, on a clear, sunny morning, when the air will be light and the sky won't be busy.

And today was the very first clear, brilliant morning they've had since their chat!

"In winter time, most winged creatures like to wait until after lunch before taking off on their daily routines", Dragonfly explained. "So we should leave after breakfast, before the air fills up with activity, flying will be more strenuous then."

Smiling to himself Little Tail did a few extra arm exercises in preparation for their big flight.

It wasn't much later that Dragonfly came over for breakfast, like she did every morning.

Soon after her recovery, feeling better and stronger, Dragonfly had moved out of Little Tail's small place and into the burrow of the old, bendy tree. The one across the clearing, where she'd first been discovered by the friendly dog.

With Little Tail's help she had turned the empty den into a warm, cosy place and set up house for herself. The place was bigger and more suitable for Dragonfly's long body and wide wings. There were no pots to be bumped over and, most importantly, Little Tail could have his cosy little bed back. Sleeping on a chair night after night was not that comfortable after all.

"Now we are neighbours", Little Tail had proclaimed with a smile. "And good neighbours and friends see each other for breakfast, lunch and dinner. We can have breakfast here, lunch at your house and dinner…" Little Tail paused, not sure how to evenly divide the three meals of the day between the two of them.

"Depending on who cooks that day?" proposed Dragonfly.

"But I always cook", noticed Little Tail.

"Because you have a better stove", smiled Dragonfly who had just begun taking cooking lessons from her friend.

On this particular morning Little Tail displayed his broadest smile when welcoming his friend.

"Good morning, Dragonfly! Let's have a quick breakfast before we set off on our journey. It is a clear morning, remember?" And he winked, busying himself at the breakfast table.

Dragonfly blinked twice, then twice more.

She clearly remembered their chat

and her promise to fly him back home on the first clear day. Although she'd had a warmer day in mind when she made the offer...

She glanced out the window, towards the little clearing surrounded by tall trees, all still bearing heavy, white cloaks. Her eyes filled with tears... probably because of the bright light outside... as she followed their trunks up, all the way to their tops which seemed to touch the sky.

Her gaze returned to her small friend humming a happy tune, laying out a huge breakfast spread.

There was dry leaf porridge sweetened with tree sap, fried mushrooms, crumpets made from baked tree bark and, to top it all, Little Tail's renowned fir tea with honey droplets on the side...

"Where had he found the honey?!"

And there were even a few insects on a stick for Dragonfly!

"Home is where the heart is... home, home, home", the dog was humming.

"You found honey?" Dragonfly blinked.

As soon as she had felt better, she too had peeked inside a few empty tree burrows, hoping to discover the remains of a bee hive and perhaps a few honey droplets left behind, a real treat in winter time. Little Tail would have never reached the dens set high into the trees, while she, with her strong wings, could do so easily.

"Oh", exclaimed Little Tail, "I've just bartered my big cooking pot for it! Best deal I've ever made! I won't be needing it much longer", smiled the dog winking again, "now that we will be leaving!"

The insect's antennae dropped.

"Which way South?" she asked herself again. There was no way of telling from down here. She will have to hover up there, high above the clearing, looking for signs that will point them in the right direction, towards warmer lands.

The sun was bright, but she knew that it was just an appearance.

The air will be frosty, with everything else still frozen in winter there will be no escaping the cold.

And as if that wasn't enough, seen from above the Snow will sparkle like thousands of twinkling stars, hurting her eyes.

Icy memories of a time when she nearly froze to death came back, making it difficult to feel brave, let alone fly around in this wintry land.

How will she find the strength to soar high, towards the tree tops? It was the first step she will have to take if she was to fly them out of this wintry place.

Will she be able to make it?

"Little Tail, I think I'll go to the old log for a little while", she whispered while stepping outside.

The dog followed shortly, bringing

two cups of steaming fir tea.

"The snow looks so happy in the sun", he noticed; "look how it smiles!"

"Not a care in the world!" murmured Dragonfly.

"It doesn't seem in the least worried that one day it will melt, turn into water and run into the ground", continued Little Tail. "Today she's just happy to be snow and to sparkle in the sunshine."

"Except that when the sun will warm up enough, its heat will pull some of the water up into the skies where it will become white fluffy clouds, like those ones", pointed Dragonfly towards the heavens above.

"Not so", contradicted Little Tail gently, "the Snow will have to wait for summer before turning into fluffy clouds. First are the grey, wintry clouds, like the ones we've had these past few days."

"No, pretty, fluffy ones like the ones flying above our heads right now", said Dragonfly taking a sip of tea.

She felt better. Maybe the tea had warmed her or maybe it was chatting with Little Tail that did the trick.

"I know summer clouds when I see them", she continued. "They are our allies. They shade the waters over which they float, making it easier for us, dragonflies, to spot any larvae or food morsel floating about. Yes, summer clouds are an ally all right!" she nodded smiling. It felt good to be reminded that up there, in the skies, there were friends as well.

Little Tail glanced towards the sky and frowned. High above their heads, across a clear patch of sky, white, cottony clouds were floating about.

"But they are summer clouds! Just like the ones..." he began then suddenly stopped, his mouth open.

The chatty dog was reduced to silence.

Dragonfly, concerned, put an arm around her friend.

"What's wrong, Little Tail?"

"C... O... M..." the dog spelled out slowly, then faster and faster, **"E, B, A, C..."** he went on, his eyes wide in wonder, studying the floating clouds.

Dragonfly followed Little Tail's gaze.

Fuzzy clouds were lazily floating above their heads, from left to right.

"Little Tail?" she questioned, turning her worried gaze towards her friend.

"They are not clouds, they are letters!" explained the dog. "Look, that's a K floating above our heads right now."

Dragonfly looked up again... and saw nothing else but a downy cloud.

"And now there's an H, an O, an M, and..." the little dog turned towards the insect.

His eyes were shining and his mouth

was stretched into the widest smile the insect had ever seen him wear.

"The clouds are spelling out words, Dragonfly!" he exclaimed while jumping off the log. He spun in circles, chasing his tail and barking madly.

When he finally stopped, panting, he pointed towards the sky again, watching his winged friend with excited eyes.

"LITTLE TAIL, **PLEASE COME BACK HOME!",** he explained slowly.

Dragonfly looked up once more and blinked, concerned. No, she couldn't see any letters and definitely no message. She shook her head in response.

"LITTLE TAIL, **PLEASE COME BACK HOME!"** cried out the dog in delight. "The message says, "LITTLE TAIL, **PLEASE COME BACK HOME!"**

"Yay!" he cheered and his four little

paws were off, frantically running around their winged companion, in a happy dance.

"It is a message..." he exclaimed, whizzing past Dragonfly. "...from my friends back home..." continued the dog when his sprint had brought him near the insect once again. "They miss me... miss me... miss me... and want me... to come home!" he panted, his tongue hanging over his bottom teeth, almost touching the ground, his bright eyes fixed upon the insect.

"When are we leaving?" he concluded.

"Oh..." the insect's voice came so soft that Little Tail had to step closer to hear it.

"I'm afraid that's a different story."

"What do you mean?" The little dog

watched Dragonfly with big eyes. He had put all his faith into his winged pal. In his heart, he was sure as snow is snow and as wood is wood, that the two of them would be able to fly back home together.

Dragonfly looked into her friend's eyes. She saw hope and trust. The flicker of a smile was still visible over the dog's face even now, when he was concerned over her own insecurities. Dragonfly did not want to disappoint her saviour and friend, yet she felt she just couldn't do it. She wasn't able to fly during icy winter days… To start with, she couldn't even tell which direction to take, to say the least!

So Dragonfly lowered her head in silence and sighed.

"And the clouds?" Little Tail pointed, smiling a hopeful little smile again.

"What about the clouds that just flew over?" He scrutinised the skies again. More downy letters seemed to be making their way above their heads.

"They are not flying, they are just drifting, my friend. There isn't a breeze in the skies today… They've been given a… push and then they drifted all the way here", sighed the insect as her gaze followed the trace of clouds.

Little Tail's eyes became watery.

Dragonfly looked up again, her gaze following the outline of the tree tops bordering their clearing, standing tall, with no wind to sway them… no wind at all.

"No wind at all?!"

The insect's eyes seemed to be growing even larger as she figured it all out. She had suddenly realized how Little

Tail's friends were helping them, all the way from their Woodland home. From far, far away!

Facing Little Tail she put her thin, front legs onto his shoulders and felt able to look into his eyes again. She smiled, grateful towards the clouds, towards this small dog with a brave heart who had left his mates behind to pursue his dream... She wouldn't have been alive if it wasn't for him, her four legged friend! And she felt grateful towards Little Tail's friends, such clever, clever creatures!

Because of them their return flight would be possible, after all!

The dog, sensing a sudden change in his friend's behaviour, was holding his breath, his heart pounding with hope. Just his tail wagged slowly.

"Your friends", the insect explained,

"they are not sending you a message!"

"They are not?" frowned the dog, "but it says my name, LITTLE TAIL."

"Yes, yes, yes, the message is addressed to you, but it has actually been flown to you, not written."

Dragonfly got up. She needed to hover about for a few seconds to stop her wings from whirring with excitement. They were making such a terrible noise! She went on explaining.

"According to the laws and regulations of flying, laws that any floating insect or device, such as a cloud, must follow, even little, fluffy clouds such as those... when someone or something flies in one direction they cannot return following the same pathway."

"Are there pathways in the skies?"

Little Tail felt a bit confused, as he'd never seen any.

"Of course there are! Otherwise we would constantly bump into each other while flying about! What it means to us", drew the insect to an end, "is that the cloudy-message must have drifted over here in a straight line, coming directly from home, your Woodland home that is. Your friends are showing you the way back! But it's not the writing or even the shape of clouds that matters. They have been blowing you a trail of pointers. They've been sending you directions home and this bread-crumb-cloud-trail leads to, or to be precise, arrives from your home, all the way here, in a straight line!" concluded the excited insect. "Boy, they surely miss you... and they're very clever too!"

But Little Tail was not around anymore. While the insect was still finishing off her conclusion the happy pawed traveller had already run inside his shelter, picked up his parcel and, without even bothering to shut the door behind him, was back.

"Ready?" his wagging tail was asking.

"Let's go!" his sparkling eyes were demanding.

"What about your door? You left it open", puzzled Dragonfly.

"The house will await the next tired traveller. I'll leave it open. One day this cosy burrow will shelter someone else just as well as it accommodated us." Little Tail held his parcel closer to his chest. "Oh, Dragonfly, I do hope my excitement hasn't made me heavier. I don't want to cause you extra trouble during our flight!"

The insect laughed.

"On the contrary, it most probably made you lighter! Don't you feel like you've grown little wings already?"

Little Tail tiptoed around feeling indeed as light as a feather. As if a tiny pair of wings had grown on his back, lifting him slightly above the ground. He giggled.

"I do feel them, Dragonfly! Who knows, maybe a pair of wings will grow on my back by the time we reach my Woodland home!" And he spun around with joy. "Let's go HOME!" he cheered, jumping onto the insect's back.

"Off we go!" came a confident answer.

"You know what, Dragonfly, I arrived here looking for Snow and found much more than I was hoping for. I finally met Snow and I've turned into a Snowdog all right, only for a few days… and nights. But, most importantly, I've found a true friend", smiled Little Tail, holding tight onto the insect's neck.

The dragonfly's wings whirred.

"You, my friend", said the dog

further. "And I'm taking you back home with me! I can't bring any snow back and I can't bring Blue either…" Little Tail paused for a second.

"Do you think he would have turned into Green, once home?" He laughed as he went on. "But if I had to travel all the way here just to have met you and bring YOU back home, well, it was all worthwhile!"

Dragonfly's wings whirred with joy.

"Good-bye, Snow", the dog waved. "Good-bye, Blue. Good-bye, Snowflakes… I shall miss being one of you. Good-bye, Snow-land, until we meet again!" From down below Snow was sending them her own good-byes by giving out her best sparkles. And a small, blue shape briefly showed itself and waved, just as the two travellers disappeared out of sight.

CHAPTER 11

SOMETHING IS COOKING

Unknown animals or people aren't always what they seem to be. They aren't always as scary or as strange as they first appear.

That's why, more often than we realize, being polite is the first step towards being friendly. And being friendly is a sure step towards making new friends.

For friends bring joy and comfort to our lives, no matter where we live, where we come from or where we go to.

Or so says The Book of Life.

Dragonfly and Little Tail flew and flew, chasing the trail of clouds.

The insect was feeling grateful for now she knew which way to fly.

Perched upon her back was the dog, his tummy full of butterflies, feeling like he was flying himself – that is, all by himself. His eyes glued to the trail ahead, hoping at every twist and turn that he will spot his beloved Woodland.

But their journey had only just begun and many adventures still lay ahead.

Their first break had been for lunch.

Little Tail felt hungry, obviously.

Dragonfly felt tired, of course. The flying exercises she had done during the past weeks had proved a walk in the park compared to the real thing, their flight so far. But the delicious food laid out by the dog, washed down with fir tea and followed by an afternoon nap had given her extra strength.

The dog was too excited to sleep. He offered to keep watch, too thrilled at the thought that he will soon see his old friends again... Summer Wind! Pete! Lizard!

What gifted friends, how they devised such a clever He examined the trail of clouds again, floating in a straight line across the sky. Their path seemed to never end. Will it still be there in the morning? He certainly hoped so.

Little Tail couldn't stop smiling to himself. How long had it taken his friends to shape so many letters?

Summer Wind was surely involved, Pete too and, knowing Lizard, yes, he would have helped as well.

What were his dear friends doing now, at this time in the afternoon? Were they resting, too? Or were they still crafting letters? If he could fly really high, high above the clouds, would he be able to spot them, his friends, sitting together at the beginning of the trail of downy-letters?

What an unusual rainbow across the sky this white path was painting!

At one end were his friends, at the other end... who knows? He and Dragonfly were somewhere in between.

How far until they will reach his Woodland home? A day? A week? He will soon have to start looking for food if the trip takes too long...

Dragonfly stretched her wings.

"That was the perfect nap, Little Tail! Thank you!"

"You're welcome!"

Spotting the cloudy trail above the insect remembered their journey. "Quick, let's be on our way! We might even get to your Woodland tonight!"

Little Tail jumped on. He felt his heart leaping ahead, already reaching his beloved forest.

The Lake will be the first landmark to lay their eyes upon. Then the beautiful, green acorn trees, the windy pathways down below and then, his friends!

Where would they be sitting right now? On the most elevated piece of land, most probably in the clearing... Will they still be there tonight, if they reach his Woodland by sunset?

But it wasn't going to happen.

It was close to sunset when the trail had narrowed, the letters further and further apart. Then it grew thinner and thinner.

At first Dragonfly thought it just looked thinner, because of the dimmed daylight. But Little Tail, his eyes still following the trail ahead, was already worried and his heart had skipped a beat or two.

First, some of the letters seemed distorted. But then, then he couldn't read them anymore, there was no message spelled across the sky but a thin line of clouds. As if the weaving of cloudy-letters had been stretched into a single string.

And then they both saw it. The trail, instead of floating over the sky was sinking somewhere down below, ahead of them. The place looked rocky, with barely any trees in sight, only a few bushes.

Dragonfly knew without asking that this couldn't have been Little Tail's Woodland. And she sensed, from the stiffness in his friend's body, that the dog was worried too.

"Shall we land and have a look? I am sure we can figure out what happened to our clouds", offered the insect.

"Yes, let's!" whispered the dog, his eyes still on the lookout.

What could have happened to their

cloudy trail?

And then, he saw it.

Something else was floating towards the sky, along the damaged trail of clouds. A trace of smoke!

"Something's cooking!" exclaimed Little Tail.

"Yes, I also think so. Something strange is happening down there."

"No, Dragonfly, I mean literally cooking, somebody down there IS cooking. Look, there's a thinner, darker trace of smoke coming up. It's from a cooking fire!"

"I hope it's a good cook!" Dragonfly licked her mouth.

"I hope it's a friendly one", whished the dog.

"There's only one way to find out.

Hold on tight, we are going to land."

And Dragonfly swiftly touched ground.

The two travellers found themselves standing on a narrow piece of open ground.

The area all around looked rocky and, with the sun now hidden by the surrounding boulders, the air felt much cooler.

Only the whirring of Dragonfly's wings could be heard. Little Tail shivered a little, but his eyes watched closely.

The trail of smoke he had spotted from high above was coming from…. "That crack in the rock, over there", he pointed then quickly covered his mouth with his paw. He signalled towards Dragonfly: "we better keep as quiet as possible."

"What are you two doing there, standing like two stones just fallen from the skies? What are you waiting for, a special invitation? Come on in, the soup's ready!" a squeaky voice shouted right behind them.

Little Tail nearly jumped out of his skin. Dragonfly whizzed herself around just in time to see a small, hairy figure disappearing behind a wall of rock.

What were they to do now?

"Where did the voice come from?" panted the dog.

"From down there, I think", shouted Dragonfly over the whirring of her wings. They always made such a terrible noise when she was nervous!

The dog narrowed his eyes, straining them to get a better look. "What did it look like?"

"I don't know, it went away so quickly. I don't even know where it disappeared to."

"Did you catch a glimpse of it?"

"Of whom?"

"Of the voice!"

"I think I did!" Dragonfly answered, unsure.

"And?!" Little Tail shivered again. Was it because of this cool, shady place?

"And what?" whispered Dragonfly taking deep breaths. If she could just stop her wings from whirring!

"What did it look like?"

"Who?"

"The voice!"

"A voice has no looks."

"The creature", whispered Little Tail

louder. "The creature to whom the voice belongs to, Dragonfly! What did it look like? Did you see it?"

"Yes I did."

"And?"

"And what?"

"What did it look like?"

"What did it look like... it looked like... hairy?"

"Harry?! Harry who? I don't know any Harry!"

"Not Harry! I don't know any Harry! Hairy, it looked hairy, it had hair all over!"

"Ooh!! Ooh? Hairy? Ooh..." Little Tail uttered, even more frightened.

The two friends huddled closer, only their eyes moving, searching around. And finally, they spotted it, a narrow entrance.

Little Tail could fit through in a tight squeeze, but Dragonfly felt concerned about her long wings.

The two friends looked at each other. What else could they do?

The night was falling quickly. They didn't have a camp fire yet, let alone a shelter and it was too late to start building either of them now. And it did smell quite inviting down that narrow entrance. Actually, the aroma of cooked food was irresistible!

Nodding in silent agreement the two travellers squeezed themselves through the crack in the stone.

Little Tail went ahead, hoping that his sharp sense of smell would warn them of any possible danger lying ahead.

Dragonfly followed suit, folding her

wings as closely to her body as possible and using her antennae to feel the walls for any possible roughness that might damage them.

They advanced in silence. As the darkness of the stone tunnel was surrounding them, all they could do was carefully place one foot forward, feel for steady ground ahead and then take another small step. A slow process. But they pressed on.

Neither of them dared make a sound.

It felt like a lengthy time of blindly finding their way through the narrow passage, but soon enough it suddenly widened, leading into a vast room which seemed to be nestled deeply inside the hill.

Little Tail and Dragonfly stopped dead in their tracks, having expected anything but the sight which unfolded before their very eyes.

A round, wide room, even wider than Dragonfly's old burrow, revealed itself.

The first sight to catch their eyes was the lively fire burning right in the centre of the chamber. A row of river stones had been placed neatly around it and, sitting on top of them like an angry king on his throne, a little red pot was simmering away.

A delightful aroma rose from it, floating over the entire space, lingering in the corners and unexpectedly making its way up the visitor's nostrils. Reminding them of just how hungry they were.

"What is this heavenly smell?" whispered Dragonfly towards her friend. For if someone could recognise a scent, any scent, it was her four legged friend.

Little Tail sniffed to the left, he sniffed to the right. He sniffed high and he sniffed low. Forgetting all about his worries he even approached the simmering pot and took one good long sniff of the delightful aroma rising from it.

"Oh, Dragonfly, I simply don't know

what to call it! It smells of roasted nuts and pinecones, of minty herbs and creamy sauces. It smells like everything I love to eat, yet nothing I can cook will ever smell this good!"

Just then the dog's stomach grumbled, echoing against the stone walls.

The two friends dared not move. What if IT heard them and IT knows they've come in?

Little Tail clutched his tummy, trying to silence any other rumble before it even had a chance to occur. Dragonfly grabbed at her stomach too, just in case. The dog's nose began to twitch in an attempt to distinguish their host's individual scent. Perhaps he will be able to locate IT...

WHERE was it?

WHAT was it?

But the aroma rising from the cooking pot proved too much, overpowering any other possible scent.

Dragonfly felt her eyes nearly popping out of her head, so hard she'd strained them, searching all around.

No-one else was in sight.

"Trying to discover the secret of my pot, are we? I'm glad you like the smell because you will have to eat the food that comes with it…"

A squeaky voice, followed by a raspy laugh, rose from behind the fire. Startled, the two friends jumped backwards. The dog's tail touched the cold rock behind, Dragonfly felt her wings bending.

"This isn't good", she thought. Her antennae were moving feverishly, instinctively feeling the space around.

Their searching eyes caught sight of a strange form ahead, but the flame's golden glare made it difficult to notice anything else.

"...if you want to make it home by tomorrow evening", the high-pitched voice went on.

"We were not trying to spy on you, honestly we weren't!" exclaimed the insect feeling guilty for having enquired about the scent in the first place.

"But it does smell sooo good!" added her companion nervously, knowing that honesty was the best policy, although his tail was now firmly tucked between his legs.

The squeaky voice moved away from the fire and the two friends finally saw to whom it belonged.

"Oh, Granny Bushcop doesn't mind a bit of nosing in her soup, in her soup, in her soup…" screeched the voice further and the same raspy laugh followed.

Dragonfly wasn't sure if she should feel scared by the hairy appearance or feel sorry for the old creature walking with the aid of a cane.

The critter tilted its head to one side, speaking further in a whiny voice.

"Oh, listen to this old hag how she makes rhymes!"

"Who is she talking to? Is there someone else in here?!" wondered Little Tail trying hard to scrutinise the lair's darkest corners. His gaze returned to the old creature with wrinkled face and big eyes which was standing near the fire, her head tilted to one side, then the other, squeaking words towards an unseen fourth companion.

Dragonfly glanced towards Little Tail, "Who is she talking to?" her eyes seemed to question. Little Tail raised an eyebrow at his friend, "I don't have a clue!" it seemed to answer.

"Come and sit here, you two", the old creature pointed her knobbly stick at two little stools nearby. Then she went on, arguing with her hidden companion.

"Should I fetch the soup bowls, Granny, or will you?" She seemed to be listening, waiting for some answer, her head tilted sideways again.

Little Tail and Dragonfly threw short glances around, eyeing each other, not sure what to believe. The old creature didn't seem to mind them, too busy arguing ahead.

"All right, you old hag, I know you can't move too fast and you're half blind. I'll get the soup bowls! I seem to be the only one doing all the work around here anyway." Then, raising her voice: "and I'm not young anymore, do you hear me?" Then laughing her hoarse laugh she nodded to herself, "well, at least I'm younger than you, if you care to know!"

Little Tail raised his shoulders towards Dragonfly and stood up.

"I'll fetch the soup bowls if it will help you. Why don't you sit and rest... Granny?"

The elderly critter turned a wrinkled face towards him. She seemed to be smiling. Little Tail saw her long, sharp teeth gleaming in the light of the fire. He shut his eyes tight, trying to chase away the scary image.

"Oh, what a fine boy you are! Bless you! I knew I wasn't doing all this for nothing!" Then the creature went on, shaking her stick towards the furthest wall of the room. "Look there, in my cupboard, bring three soup bowls and three spoons. Old Granny will have some soup too. Want to see if I've made it good enough for the likes of you two!"

Little Tail took one step towards the

cupboard then stopped. He seemed to be pondering over something.

"Well, what are you waiting for? Get those bowls!" The cane thumped on the ground, the squeaky voice sounding impatient.

"Am I to bring only three bowls? What about your sister?"

The wrinkled face turned towards him, eyes narrowed in attention. "Who?!" the squeak was loud and clear, echoing in the big space underground.

"Your sister, the one you talked to earlier. Won't she be joining us for supper?"

Although it seemed impossible to the two friends, the creased face wrinkled itself even more. A raspy chuckle filled the surrounding space, echoing again and again, louder and louder. The small dog covered his ears. Dragonfly's antennae flattened. The old soul was shaking with laughter on her little stool, her bushy tail moving to and fro, her cane wobbling alarmingly.

"She will fall…" thought Dragonfly. "No, she won't… Oh, she certainly will… no, no, she won't…"

"What am I to do now?" wondered Little Tail, still half way towards the cupboard.

Eventually the laugh died away and the old creature used her bushy tail to wipe the tears from her eyes.

"Oh, what a funny little boy you are!" She waved one arm around, showing them her place. A little cupboard with pots and pans, a pantry stuffed with nuts, a little bed tucked away in a corner, a pile of old, leafy books, some needlework and the welcoming fire in the middle.

"Do you see anyone else around? There's only me living here, Granny Bushcop. I'm not having a sister. I just chat to myself, helps me pass the time." Then she pointed her cane to the three chairs around the fire, "me, myself and I!" And she laughed again.

"But you said..." Dragonfly wondered.

The squirrel turned a smiling face towards the insect, "Yes, my child?"

The insect wasn't sure how to bring up the matter. "You said... you said..." her voice died away in a whisper, "that you are the youngest one?"

The old squirrel smiled, "Of course I am. I am the third one: first is me, then myself and then I, the youngest one, see?" Her eyes twinkled as she turned towards the dog. "How many bowls, young man?"

Little Tail grinned for he had understood why Granny Bushcop thought of herself to be the youngest one.

"Three, Ma'am!"

Dragonfly still looked uncertain, staring in turns from one stool to the next, counting on her legs, because dragonflies do not have fingers.

The nut-cutter picked up the wooden spoon and stirred the pot, nodding to herself: "Yes, this is just what you two need." And then she nodded some more, approving of the aroma rising above.

For the next few minutes only the spoons chattered, for the food was too good for words. Or were the two friends too hungry? Even Old Granny was quiet, only her head nodding after each spoonful.

Once the plates were empty the two travellers' eyes were next to speak, smiling with contentment. The old squirrel, her bowl resting in her lap, seemed to have dozed off.

Little Tail stretched his legs and yawned.

Dragonfly stretched her wings. She looked at her friend with inquiring eyes. "How do you think she knew we were coming?" she whispered.

The dog shrugged his shoulders, giving another yawn. Did it really matter? They had a warm place to spend the night and their tummies were full. Without mentioning that there was a lot of that delicious soup left over for a second round in the morning. Little Tail wondered if Granny Bushcop will ever tell him the secret of her cooking.

"The clouds!"

The squeak took them both by surprise. Dragonfly turned a stunned face towards their host. The dog stopped in the middle of a yawn, his mouth wide open, his arms stretched out.

Old bushy tail seemed half asleep, her arms folded over her chest, her chin lowered, her big eyes almost closed. Yet she was talking.

"The clouds told me you two were coming... One sunny morning, as I was doing my rounds looking for nuts... for one must always look around for fallen nuts, always, that's the secret to a well stuffed pantry. One sunny winter morning I saw strange clouds floating over my head."

The squirrel's eyes were wide open now, her right paw stretched high above her head, moving in a straight line, following some imaginary clouds.

The two friends were closely following them too.

"...strange clouds," the squirrel repeated, "...for they were summer clouds on an icy, winter sky! I thought it to be a sign. A sign that must be looked into... deciphered!" And the old squirrel dropped her cane to the floor with a loud bang.

The two friends sprang from their little stools.

The story-teller smiled. She straightened her back, lifting both her arms above her head. Her eyes were looking up, twinkling.

"So Old Granny climbed to the top of the tallest tree, just like she used to during her youth."

"Which one is the tallest tree?" questioned Little Tail.

"Shh!" hissed Dragonfly.

"Why, it is this one!" smiled Granny Bushcop as she went on. "Old Granny climbed and climbed, keeping one eye on the branches, one eye on the clouds and one eye open for acorns…"

"Three eyes?" whispered Dragonfly towards the dog. But it was Little Tail's turn to frown her to silence.

The squirrel was standing now, arms stretched high above her head. With eyes shining in excitement, her face looked a lot less wrinkled and her fur was glowing red beside the fire. She didn't appear as old anymore.

"And when Old Granny reached the top, the clouds were within her reach!"

The tree rat closed up her fist, as if she had caught something. "Old Granny held the message tight and as she did so she felt it soaring in her hand like a kite in the wind. Old Granny read the message and she knew right away that she had to help."

"How did she know?" Dragonfly nudged Little Tail.

The squirrel smiled then nodded. "Old Granny knows her forest... for she has lived here all her life. This is the oldest forest in the world and the biggest one. Nobody can cross it in one day. So Old Granny knew that she would have to help the travellers cross it on their way home."

"How did she know there will be more than one to travel? The message was only addressed to you!" interrupted the insect again, whispering loudly.

The old nut-cutter sighed and narrowed her eyes while glancing towards the chatterbox.

"I didn't. But I was hoping that, whoever the message was addressed to, wouldn't embark on such a long journey all alone."

Then looking up towards her closed fist she went on.

"So Old Granny caught the first cloud and tugged."

"At first, it wasn't easy to pull it off its path, but Old Gran was determined to help. She tugged again and again, until the cloud came down from the skies. The next one followed it, then another one and another. Now it was just a matter of keeping the ball rolling. So Old Granny stood on the top of the tallest tree from the oldest forest in the world... and spun clouds. She spun many clouds that day,

Old Gran she did and as soon she had a ball of cloudy yarn which was big enough, she would drop it to the ground and start spinning another one."

Dragonfly jumped off his chair.

"That's why the message had disappeared from the skies! She took it!" Thrilled by her own discovery the insect forgot all about her manners or about the place where they found themselves. Taking one brave step towards the old creature, she demanded, "Where are they? What have you done with them?"

Little Tail half rose from his seat in an attempt to calm his friend.

The old furry squirrel smiled and pointed towards the furthest corner of her burrow. There, by the wall, lay a row of white balls. Not wool, as Dragonfly first imagined, but clouds spun into balls! The insect went closer. Was she imagining it? Were the balls quivering? She dared not touch them. Until one of them, the closest one, vibrated suddenly and brushed against her wing. Dragonfly jumped out of her skin.

"They are alive!" she screamed.

The squirrel laughed. "Of course they are! I've only just spun them, but if I let them go they will be ready to float and follow their course again. I will do so in the morning, for they've served their purpose. They've brought you here, haven't they?"

Little Tail jumped up and hugged the old nut collector.

The insect was still trying to understand what happened and why, in the end, they had to thank the furry creature?

"Don't you understand", whispered

the dog, "we wouldn't have made it through this forest in one go. We simply had to stop over for a rest and a meal." And he licked his mouth. "By climbing to the top of the tallest tree Old Granny risked her own life to save us." And he hugged the aged squirrel again. The nut-cutter affectionately wrapped her bushy tail around the small dog. To the stunned insect it looked as if her four legged friend had disappeared entirely in a mass of red wool. Dragonfly stepped closer, her head lowered.

"I am sorry for doubting you, Gran. Thank you."

The squirrel smiled and nodded. But it wasn't time for chit-chat and she knew it. Little Tail slowly picked up the cane and handed it to her, his eyes filled with awe.

The old nut-cutter clapped her

hands.

"Time for bed! Help yourselves to some rugs and come sleep by the fire. I'll make sure you're up at sunrise. We will have breakfast and then you can be on your way in no time!"

CHAPTER 12

LITTLE TAIL COMES BACK

Lending a helping hand always proves to be just as beneficial to the assistant as it is to the assisted. Because helping someone often opens a door towards amazing opportunities for both parties involved.

Never forget that home is where your heart is and that you can always rely on your heart to show you the way home. If lost, let your heart be your true North.

Or so says The Book of Life.

The two travellers and Old Granny Bushcop all enjoyed a cheerful breakfast the following morning.

Little Tail insisted on making some of his very own fir tea, which the squirrel liked very much. So when Little Tail offered her the remainder of the fir leaves he had brought along, the old nut-cutter shared with him the secret of her cooking.

"Just as a token of my appreciation", she explained, "for your fir tea is the best I've ever tasted and you've gifted the last of it to me", she smiled and Dragonfly was sure she had spotted the glint of a tear between the squirrel's long eyelashes. Little Tail promised to return soon and bring her even more tea, for there were LOTS of fir trees in his Woodland.

"Everything packed?"

Old Granny Bushcop did not like long good-byes.

"Long good-byes make for difficult journeys. Brief and sweet ones make even the longest journey seem short."

"All packed. Got Dragonfly, myself…" Little Tail counted.

"Am I to be packed now?" worried the insect, her wings whirring a little as they always did when she became agitated… Or when she was excited… Or when she wasn't sure what to do… She couldn't imagine Little Tail travelling home all on his own, carrying her all wrapped up in a bundle! And what about her wings?!

The small dog laughed. Old Granny Bushcop chuckled. Dragonfly frowned.

"What's so funny?"

"Oh, my friend, I am not going to

turn you into a parcel! How will I fly the rest of the journey home? But you are the most important one in our journey, so of course you're getting first place on the packing list. And then myself. Got Dragonfly and I. See?" smiled the dog.

The insect disagreed. Her antennae quivered.

"You said got Dragonfly and myself, not got Dragonfly and I."

Little Tail sighed. The squirrel chuckled. The insect lifted her eyebrows. Why did the others always find her questions amusing?

Old Granny walked slowly to her cupboard and came back carrying something wrapped tightly in a leaf.

"My dear Dragon which flies", she addressed the insect while opening the package.

A sweet smell tickled everyone's nostrils. The squirrel closed her eyes for a second, in appreciation towards the precious content of her bundle. Little Tail felt his mouth water. Dragonfly sensed her discomfort melting away.

Out of the tightly wrapped bundle the squirrel took out a...

Little Tail's mouth stretched into a smile and a tiny drop of saliva fell to the floor. Dragonfly's eyes grew even larger and the shape of a smile appeared on her face.

She took out a cookie!

Skilfully she broke it in three.

"Here's me", and she gave the insect the first piece. "Here's myself", she spoke as she gave the dog the second piece. "And here's I", she concluded, keeping the third piece to herself. "All parts of the same whole."

"But different parts!" exclaimed the insect, her eyes twinkling now with understanding.

"Friends", completed the dog.

The squirrel smiled and nodded in response then turned towards the dog.

"Got everything?"

Little Tail was busy licking the last cookie crumbs off his paws. So he signalled a YES excitedly, by making use of his eyebrows.

"...and my parcel", he cautiously went on, picking up where he'd left off before Dragonfly's interruption. "The one I brought from home. It will hold enough food for the last bit of the trip."

The dog paused, contemplating his parcel. Bending over, he fumbled with something. "I won't be needing these anymore", he spoke softly, taking out his hand-carved nut shells and handing them to Old Gran. The squirrel's bushy tail swished, her pointy ears stood up.

"For me? These are the most beautiful tea cups I ever saw. Thank you!" She carefully placed them in her cupboard, in the same place where the tightly wrapped package containing the cookie had laid. Then she stepped back to admire them.

"And we're ready to roll!" exclaimed Little Tail. On a second thought he quickly corrected himself, "to fly, we're ready to fly!"

Dragonfly, who was just about to speak, closed her mouth and headed for the exit.

Choosing one of the cloud balls she started rolling it out of the burrow. Little Tail followed closely, rolling a second one. Old Granny Bushcop came last, bringing the third ball.

Out in the morning sun the air felt fresh and the insect enjoyed opening her wings again, stretching them, preparing them for the flight.

The balls of cloud were bouncing on the spot.

"They can sense they're in open air again", smiled the squirrel. "There, there", she patted one. "I'll set you free as soon as these two are ready. Just remember to fly home now, all three of you", she seemed to be scolding the shivering balls. And Dragonfly was sure she saw one of them bouncing a little faster, as if nodding in agreement!

But before she could say anything Gran was speaking again, smiling encouragingly. The insect had learned to like the bushy smile and twinkling eyes, for whenever they happened together something good always followed. And this morning they made the insect feel confident about the journey ahead.

The squirrel addressed her guests:

"And you, you follow the cloudy trail. All the way home!"

Suddenly a heavy cough started to shake the old creature and soon enough she waved the travellers off with a swipe of her paw.

In no time at all Little Tail had jumped on Dragonfly's back again and they were off!

Carefully, the squirrel bit off the string holding the first downy ball together. Like a snake uncoiling itself the trail of clouds straightened and took for the skies.

"Whoosh!"

The two friends were flying now, going round and round the tallest tree of the oldest forest in the world, curious to see for themselves how high the Old Squirrel had climbed... when a white arrow rushed pass them, pushing ahead.

"Did you see that?" exclaimed Little Tail just as Dragonfly regained her balance. "It was the first ball of clouds!"

And up, up, up they soared, flying round and round still, up and up until the nut-cutter's red and bushy tail looked almost like a flower petal on the rocky ground below.

Their hearts filled with admiration towards their new friend as they realized how high she had climbed to simply help two strangers.

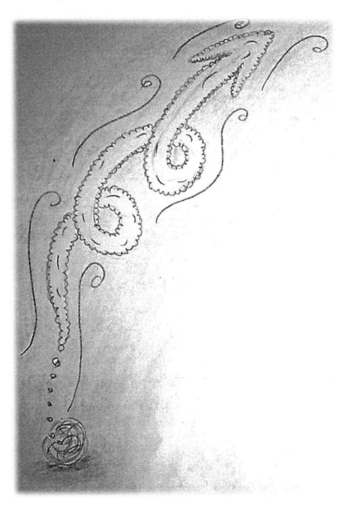

A second white arrow sped past them.

"Zoom!"

Dragonfly looked around. Little Tail looked down.

"Watch out, here comes the third one!"

"Vuum!"

From so high up it was now easy for our traveller friends to spot the end of the forest and the direction the cloudy trail had just taken.

"That way!" exclaimed Dragonfly. And they were gone!

Flying over the squirrel's forest was like flying over a sea of green. The trees were like rough waves rising to the sky, while the bushes and the rocks formed patches of calm sea in between.

"Wee!" exclaimed Dragonfly after a while, rising above the wavy trees. "Look, Little Tail, there's the beach!"

The dog squinted a little, searching far ahead.

A yellow line seemed to be bordering the forest, becoming more and more distinct as they approached it. Widening, like a strip of golden sand along the sea shore.

Could it be true? Was it for real?

Just as he was marvelling about the unexpected beach ahead the dog noticed something very peculiar about this strip of sand. It seemed to have a life of its own, for it was shifting, shimmering in the sun.

"Dragonfly!" he called out, "let's not land there yet… Could you fly us a little closer instead? This isn't sand. Sand doesn't sway like this! That yellow strip ahead is... moving!"

Dragonfly nodded, for she too had noticed the movement ahead.

"What was it?"

The insect's sharp eyes were now

searching for a safe landing spot. There were too many trees and bushes on this side of the yellow strip, no space for a safe landing. "Perhaps on the other side?" She tried to peer across the swaying beach.

It was then that it all happened.

Very fast.

Something touched one of her wings. It mostly just brushed past it. But that's all it took for Dragonfly to lose her balance and plunge, head first, into a crash-landing.

For a brief second the insect felt worried-sick about her friend. She had crashed landed many times before, but Little Tail had not.

"Bump!"

"Zduf!"

"Crash!"

"Ouch!"

"Help!"

Then silence...

Dragonfly was lying flat on her tummy, underneath a yellow roof.

"Little Tail?" she called out.

More silence.

Just the swaying hum, all around.

"Why wasn't her friend answering? Was he hurt? Was he in danger?"

Dragonfly got herself up and, before she even checked for injuries, she looked around, searching for the dog. But it was in vain for tall stems were growing everywhere, blocking her view.

"Little Taaaaaail!" she yelled, panicking. She gazed up. Very high up, between towering stalks, she could make out a patch of blue sky.

Oh, forget about the fall and the myriad of plants growing so close together! She will have to make her way up there, where she could soar above them all.

She had to find Little Tail!

Choosing the thickest stalk around Dragonfly started climbing. Higher and higher, until she reached the top. Carefully she made her way onto its flat platform and soon enough she could feel the wind against her wings and the warm sunshine on her body. She felt more confident now.

It would be just a matter of seconds before she could take off and, as soon as she can be airborne, she will have a good look around. Little Tail must be somewhere nearby. He would have touched the ground before her, for he was heavier...

Now, from which way did they come, again?

The insect stretched her neck, trying to spot the forest. The view spreading before her eyes took her breath away.

As far as Dragonfly could see an ocean of yellow was slowly swaying in the sun.

The yellow tops seemed to be graciously floating above the ground, so gentle was their movement. The insect watched in awe until she realized that she, too, was sitting on a yellow dome. She looked at her feet. A gold powder was covering them. It was sweet and sticky and Dragonfly realized at once what it was.

"Pollen!"

She looked again at the yellow sea ahead.

"Daisies!"

As far as her eyes could see there were daisy flowers!

They had crash-landed in a field of daisies!

"What a stroke of luck", thought Dragonfly. "Daisies are some of the friendliest flowers in the world. Why, they even have friendly visitors." She started counting them on her legs.

"**Butterflies**, for example! They always obey the rules of flying and they like to keep to themselves."

She put up another leg.

"**Ladybugs**! Just as the name suggests, Ladies of flight, always polite."

She put up the next leg.

"**Beetles**! Bit noisy, but at least you hear them coming. Otherwise, harmless."

Confident of her counting so far, the insect put up another leg and opened her mouth, ready to speak. But no name came out. Dragonfly frowned. She knew there must be another insect, she just knew it!

"A-ha!" she exclaimed triumphantly. "**Spiders**!" She gave a little shiver. "Better watch out for their webs!"

She then put up another leg, thought for a second then nodded.

"No, can't think of anyone else. That's all of them!" She checked out her four outstretched legs while balancing carefully, a little puzzled.

"Weren't there supposed to be five insects? Oh, but of course! ME! I'm the fifth one! **Dragonflies!**"

Content with her list, the insect

prepared her wings for take-off.

"And now, to look for Little Tail!" She gave a little laugh while putting out yet another counting leg, "dogs!"

"Haven't you forgotten someone?" a crystal clear voice came through.

Dragonfly spun around on her daisy, a bit too fast and the flower head swayed. But she managed to steady herself, her wings whizzing. Only then did she look beyond.

Just next door, sitting on a neighbouring flower, was a round, stripy, black and yellow...

"Bee..." whispered Dragonfly in horror.

"I believe that's number... seven?" added the striped insect, smiling sweetly.

Dragonfly felt her legs shake. Bees... bees were friendly, sometimes. Most of the time unless, unless... one caught them on the wrong foot. What did that even mean? She glanced at the bee's feet. Six of them! How will she know which one is the wrong foot?!

"Heeeelp", the word came out without Dragonfly even realising she uttered it.

The bee smiled again.

"Too sweetly", Dragonfly thought, starting to see yellow and black patterns everywhere.

"Yes, I need your help! How kind of you to offer it!"

The stripy jacket paused for a moment and Dragonfly thought she saw a tear rolling down the bee's furry cheeks.

When the bee began talking again her big eyes were full of sadness.

"Allow me to introduce myself. I am B-Bee, pleased to meet you." And, sure-footed, she stepped to the edge of her flower, outstretching a foreleg.

Dragonfly rubbed her arms nervously. "Shake hands with a bee? But if I don't..." and her wings whizzed. So very cautiously Dragonfly stepped towards the edge of her own flower head. It only tilted a little. Then, as quick as she could, she closed her eyes and shook the outstretched arm.

"I am Dragonfly..." she uttered.

It felt like a very long handshake and soon enough Dragonfly realized that she was actually trying to free her own leg out of the grasp of the cunning bee... which had it stuck onto her own.

"What is happening?!" Dragonfly panicked. "What are you doing?! Let me go!" the green insect cried, turning even greener.

"I can't believe you're scared! You're the Water Witch, if anyone should be scared it should be me", replied the bee pulling away her own limb and so freeing them both. "It's just good, old pollen. Sticky, remember? Sorry, can't help it. Pollen just sticks to my body." And she dusted herself off. A tiny yellow cloud appeared all around her. It smelled sweet and Dragonfly recognised it as such, pollen.

"I am the Water what?" It was the Damselfly's turn to ask questions.

"We call your species Water Witches. You know, because you love water so much and it never seems to harm you."

The Dragonfly's wings shimmered a little. "Water!" she thought, excitedly. She missed it so much! Remembering the lake Little Tail had told her about she realized she was yet to find her lost friend! But just as she opened her mouth to speak, the bee went on.

"Look at all these daisies, swaying so peacefully under the bright sun. Without a care in the world, one would believe. Wouldn't they?" And the bee nodded towards the yellow sea.

"Is she waiting for an answer?" Dragonfly agonised. "What if I don't give her the correct answer, will she sting me then...? Oh, what should I say? Yes... No..." Dragonfly tried to mumble a neutral "uh-hmm".

The bee went on.

"Oh, but they do worry. Can't you hear them? Give us the breath of life... the breath of life..."

Dragonfly held her own breath, trying hard to listen. She couldn't hear a thing! Well, nothing besides the swishing noise the flowers were making under the soft breeze. And the bee's voice. Dragonfly shook her head, perhaps her ears were blocked? She tried to unclog them by heating her temples gently, first the left one, then the right one. Still, she couldn't hear the flowers talk.

"What are you doing?" the bee

quizzed.

"I'm trying to unblock my ears. I can't hear the flowers talk", Dragonfly admitted, still shaking her head.

The stripy-jacket smiled. "Flowers don't speak out loud, like we do. They speak... to me. You have to read their body language."

Noticing the puzzled look on the Dragonfly's face the bee went on.

"Watch them sway. A bit too much for the amount of breeze blowing about, isn't it? It's because their heads are so heavy, heavy with pollen. They need to be pollinated. They WANT to be pollinated."

"But you are here..."

"Yes, I am, but I am all alone. I got here... by accident, you see, much earlier in the season than the rest of my folk.

To find the flowers already in bloom!" B-Bee sighed. "I remember stories like this being told ever since I was little. It has happened in the past too, that the flowers bloomed earlier in the year. Because the earth heats up, you see. Spring happens earlier and earlier. Only my folk aren't in the habit of migrating so early in the season in order to pollinate..."

"Is that so important?"

"Pollinating is the breath of life! Without it the plants won't bear any fruit or produce any seeds and there won't be any honey either. Or bees!"

The bee stopped for a second, watching the green insect with pleading eyes. "This is why I need YOUR help!"

Dragonfly thought of the cool lake waiting for her at the end of the journey. She thought of Little Tail too. But B-Bee seemed in trouble. What should she do? Oh, how she wished the dog was here! He always seems to make the right decision!

"I'll help you", she felt her mouth speak almost before her mind had even decided what to do.

It just felt like the right thing, to offer help.

The bumble bee buzzed around happily.

"Then let's do it!"

"Do what?"

"Pollinate the flowers, of course! The job will take half the time if we do it together."

Dragonfly looked around, stunned. There were… so many flowers she couldn't even count!

It will take them forever! More than forever, forever and ever!

Instead, she just asked, "How do I pollinate?"

"Watch me!" and B-bee quickly demonstrated. "You sit on a flower. Make sure you sit on the golden cushion that forms the central part. You roll yourself in pollen. You move to another flower and do the same. It is as simple as that!"

Forgetting all her worries, Dragonfly smiled. Pollinating looked easy and fun. And pretty quick too. Before she knew it she was sitting, rolling, flying to the next flower, sitting, rolling, moving on. Bouncing from flower to flower to flower to Little Tail to flower...

"Little Tail?!" Dragonfly almost lost her balance. She whizzed herself back in place.

In the middle of the daisy field, quietly looking up, holding his ears like two big petals around his head, sat Little Tail!

"Little Tail!" Dragonfly exclaimed excitedly. "I…"

"Shhh or she'll hear you", whispered the four legged creature.

"Who?" questioned the insect and on noticing the alarmed look on her friend's face she quickly whispered, "Who?"

"The bee!" mouthed Little Tail, listening carefully. "Hear how she buzzes. She's upset! She might even sting us both! Do like me, pretend you're a flower until she flies away. Quick, here she comes!"

And Little Tail froze, looking straight up, his ears held high, level with his face.

Dragonfly let herself drop onto a nearby flower, pollinating as best as she could. Maybe B-Bee won't notice her friend.

"So, will your friend help us? What did he say?" the bee smiled sweetly.

Dragonfly's eyes nearly popped out of her head with surprise. But the bee had no time to chat. She just instructed over her shoulder:

"If he runs towards sunrise, where the flowers face, he can shake off the pollen onto the nearby flowers. But only run towards sunrise, mind you. Then he will have to walk slowly back and then do another row of daisies, running towards sunrise again." And she busily buzzed away.

"Thank you, little brown flower!" she called out, once more encompassed in a cloud of gold dust.

Little Tail dared not move, just his eyes blinked.

As soon as the bee was out of earshot Dragonfly explained to her friend everything the stinger had told her. Especially that she wasn't as threatening as everybody believed her to be! Quite the contrary, there was a genuine sweetness in her smile...

For the rest of the day B-Bee buzzed, Dragonfly whizzed and Little Tail ran one way, then walked back, then ran some more. But eventually the task had been completed and the entire daisy field was pollinated!

Little Tail collapsed to the ground at the edge of the meadow. Dragonfly sat on a blade of grass nearby. It felt good to sit on something green and non-sticky for a while.

"My legs are sooo tired!" exclaimed the dog. "But you know what, Dragonfly, it feels good to have helped B-Bee and the flowers!"

Dragonfly nodded in agreement. She had some pollen stuck to her mouth and she was trying her best to clean it off. Only as soon as it was off her mouth it would stick to one of her forelegs. And to take it off her forelegs she had to use her hind legs or her mouth. Then the pollen would stick further and further again.

"Sticky business!" complained Dragonfly.

B-Bee whizzed herself nearby. "My friends, what you did today nobody has ever done before! This story will stick to the bee's history like… honey!"

"Like pollen!" smiled Dragonfly crookedly, still fighting to clean off the last grain.

"Thank you both so much! I wish I could repay you in some way…" Then she advised Dragonfly, "Use water, pollen always comes off with water."

Dragonfly sighed and her wings dropped. The very word of the most sought after substance in the world was making her drool. "I wish I could, but where will I find water here?" and she shrugged her shoulders helplessly.

B-Bee buzzed excitedly. "Water is

but a flap of wings away, my friend! This way!" And she took off, calling out from the heights of the sky, "Follow me!"

Dragonfly, in her rush to take off, forgot all about the grain of pollen stuck to her leg. Little Tail just ran happily after his two winged companions. He could definitely do with a swim!

B-Bee had long darted away, but Dragonfly's wing span was no match and soon the two insects were flying side by side. Right on their heels was Little Tail, his eyes trained onto the big, bright wings of his friend, much easier to follow than the tiny bee.

For a distant spectator it looked more like the dog was chasing the insects.

"Really, why would you believe something like that?" a deep voice exclaimed. "No dog in this world would chase a bee! A Dragonfly maybe, if I come to think of it, for a bit of fun, perhaps. But a bee? Let's be serious! Rather the other way around!"

"You mean a Dragonfly to chase a bee?" another voice joined in, sounding rather high-pitched as it spoke after the first one, low and resonant.

"Oh, oh, I know, I know!" a third voice, an excited voice, emerged.

"Yes, Pete?" the resonating voice spoke calmly, sounding rather doubtful.

"A bee chasing a dog!" the excited voice exclaimed.

"That is correct!" the deep voice accepted the answer.

The three spectators were sitting further to one side, away from the daisy field for it made the one named Pete sneeze. All that pollen would get into his trunk, blocking it and giving him the sneezes.

"I've never seen that bee before..." the deep voice whispered thoughtfully, "and I should know most creatures living in our Woodland, shouldn't I? She must have flown here from far away."

"Must have been the heat wave that has brought her here", the high pitched voice replied.

"You're quite right, Murphy, you're quite right."

The one named Murphy went on. "Haven't seen that Dragonfly around either."

The excited voice, answering to the name of Pete, quickly joined in.

"Must have flown here from far away." Then he added hurriedly, while he still had a turn to speak: "haven't seen that d... d... d..."

"Dog, Pete, it is a dog. Yes, you were saying?" the deep voice encouraged him.

The excited voice suddenly sounded over the moon and Pete, its owner, jumped off the Rock, running after the dog.

"I have seen this dog before! I have, I have! It's Little Tail! Little Taaaaaaaail!

You're back! You're back!"

"Little Tail?" the resounding voice rumbled.

"Little Tail!" the high pitched voice exclaimed.

And the other two spectators, Summer Wind and Murphy the lizard, hurriedly followed in their friend's leaps.

A funny procession reached the shore of the lake.

A bee and a dragonfly...

...chased by a dog...

...which seemed to be chased by a toy elephant...

...chased in turn by a lizard who sat on a leaf...

...carried at top speed, through the air, by the zephyr!

The serene surface of the lake soon filled with tiny ripples as the gush of wind approached.

The little dog smiled. In his haste to catch up with his two winged companions he hadn't even taken the time to look around. But now, that they stopped, he seemed to recognise his surroundings! The majestic acorn trees neighbouring the water, the lake with its ripples…

"Its ripples?" Little Tail couldn't believe his eyes. "Then that meant that… that…" he spun on his heels, looking behind him. He didn't have to look far for as soon as he had spun around something else came rushing towards him and, having just caught up with him,

"Fa-thud!"

It collided!

"Little Tail! Little Tail!" the yellow shape exclaimed, over the moon with joy!

"Pete?" The dog couldn't believe his eyes, nor his ears!

But he knew he was right. It was his dear friend Pete, the yellow toy elephant. How very much like Pete to have bumped into him!

A laugh and a hug later Murphy and Summer Wind have also reached the lake.

What a happy reunion!

The Summer Wind blew a swirl of daisy petals around his long departed friend to welcome him back and Lizard promised not to poke his blue tongue at neither B-Bee nor Dragonfly – and in any case he liked ants better!

The warm summer evening had soon fallen over their gathering but frequent bouts of laughter and a happy chit-chat could be heard until late in the night.

And it is said that the bee community living near Little Tail's Woodland still tell their young ones, even to this day, amazing stories of a pollinating dog and dragonfly, of great bravery and good friendship between a dog, a lizard, a yellow toy elephant, a squirrel, the Wind and... well, the Snow. Of course, Lizard soon enjoyed his morning dreams again and Pete, his ice-cream flavoured clouds.

"Whoosh..."

The End

More Books by this Author

Joyful Trouble

Based on the True Story of a Dog
Enlisted in the Royal Navy

UK Amazon Bestseller in Children's
eBooks, Historical Fiction

UK Amazon Bestseller in Young Adult,
Historical Fiction

UK Amazon Most Gifted Paperback,
Children's

"Well written! In an age where we often

struggle to get children to read this is a wonderful book!" (Amazon Review)

"A winning tale for children and dog lovers of all ages" (Susan Day, Author, Illustrator)

Chapter 1
The Dog Parade

'Chase you to the dogs, Tommy!' shouted Ana, rushing ahead.

'Doggies, doggies!' The little boy trailed behind her, red in the face.

He was clutching his own stuffed dog by the tail, his eyes intent on his sister.

The sailor hat on his head flew off. He did not notice it. Or maybe he did, but was too happy to be without.

Ana slowed down her pace, knowing

her little brother would not catch up with her. He was almost five; she was nine. They would often race, but she would always wait for him. Like now.

She shielded her eyes from the sun, remembering her mother doing the same. She felt big whenever she could do something just like her mom.

Her brother ran towards her with the full strength of a little boy. His hair was wild now, ruffled by the wind. Grandma wouldn't like it. They must always wear hats in the sun.

She liked to look after her little brother.

Luckily Grandad came behind.

He stopped by the fallen hat and sighed. He bent slowly and painfully picked it up. He shook off the dust and put it on his own head.

Tommy was still busy running. He was looking at his feet. He had new shoes and they were too big. So he was watching his feet, believing that this prevented him from tripping and falling.

That's why he hasn't noticed his sister had stopped.

End of extract.

Take home an unbelievable and humorous true story of an incredible dog and how he found his true, yet unexpected calling. You will love the moving tale of Joyful Trouble, a dog whose love for humans went beyond any human-dog connection. When a Great Dane arrives in a Navy base nobody expects him to win everybody's hearts, although breaking some rules along the way.

"A book that reads like a movie!"(Amazon Review)

"It sparkles with good, old fashioned family time and family storytelling, treasured childhood moments that sadly get lost too often in this fast-paced world. The young reader will quickly warm up to the young children in the story as they learn about a very special Great Dane as well as a vital part of their grandfather's past. This is a

compassionate and heart-warming story"
(Reader's Favorite Review)

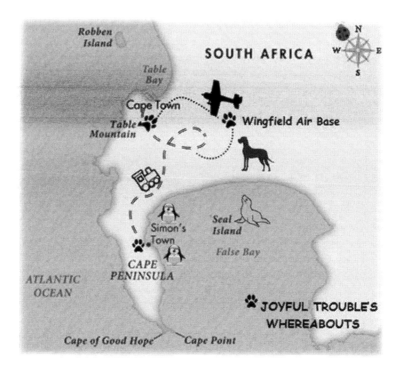

On this map you can follow Joyful
Trouble and his many adventures
Can you find the friendly insect following
Joyful Trouble in his adventures? She's
hiding in every picture.
In America she's known as a Ladybug.
In Britain she's known as a Ladybird.

More Books by this Author

Puppy

12 Months of Rhymes and Smiles

From fun and playful to creative and crafty, Patricia Furstenberg's musical rhymes express all the adoring and amusing happenings that puppies just happen to fall into when they enter our household, especially if children are present. With bright and humorous illustrations this is a book that children and grown-ups will love reading over and over.

APRIL

When a Puppy Is Born

A little whimper, a lot of love.

Sleeping tight, drinking milk.

A bitsy **tongue** to taste the world,

A brand new puppy has been born.

A toy, **so small**, with fur of silk.

A tiny ear; to flick and hear.

A tiny **heart** that beats so fast.

A **mother**'s cuddle is all he needs.

Hush, little **puppy**, sleep and dream

Of milk, your brothers and lots of love.

And games to play, places to explore,

Your life's ahead of you, hush now.

And puppy sleeps and sucks and dreams,

He listens now, for one last time.

Soon he'll explore his brand new life

And only listen when... fast asleep.

Why do we love the **puppy** so?

Because he's soft and smells so sweet?

Because he trusts us so complete?

Puppies are **miracles** with fur.

Puppies are promise of new life,

They bring us **laughter**, they don't bear grudge.

Puppies are perfect balls with **tails**,

Puppies love life and don't ask much.

End of this sample.

A great gift for any occasion, but especially a unique gift for birthdays, dog lovers and graduation. ***Puppy: 12 Months of Rhymes and Smiles*** has a loving and innocent message that will endure for lifetimes.

E-Book and Paperback available from all Amazon stores online.

Universal link: Mybook.to/Puppy

Mybook.to/JoyfulTrouble

LARGE PRINT Edition:
Mybook.to/JoyfulTroubleLP

Acknowledgements and Note from the Author

My thanks go to lovely Jenny Dwight for her swift, professional and friendly service.

Twitter: @JenInspire, E-mail: inspireproofreading@gmail.com

Pete does exist and he looks just as you see him on the cover of this book. He is the inspiration behind these stories and often looked over my shoulder during the process. I hope that you will enjoy reading them just as much as I enjoyed writing them.

About the Author

Patricia Furstenberg came to writing though reading, her passion for books being something she inherited from her parents.

She loves to write children's stories and poems about amazing animals. She believes each creature has a story and a voice, if only we stop to listen.

Patricia is passionate about children's rights and she often writes on this topic for **The Huffington Post South Africa.** She also pens the **"Sunday Dog Tales"** column for mypuppyclub.net, a website for dog lovers. She has her own blog, **Alluring Creations, http://alluringcreations.co.za/wp/**

Patricia was one of the winners of the Write Your Own Christie Competition. The Judges (Mathew Prichard, David

Brawn, Harper Collins UK and Daniel Mallory, Harper Collins US) "were impressed by her thorough investigation and admired the strength of her narrative"

One of the characters portrayed in her children's story "Happy Friends" is Pete, the yellow toy elephant. Not many know, but Pete exists and lives in Pat's home.

This Romanian born writer is living happily with her husband, children and dogs in sunny South Africa.

Printed in Great Britain
by Amazon

46196179R00213